Being up on the diving platform during the day was one thing. But at night, in the darkness and silence, it was a completely different experience. It was scary and exciting at the same time. Jessica recognized the sensation with a shock—it was almost the same feeling she had when her boyfriend, Sam Woodruff, kissed her. It was a delicious, exhilarating feeling.

Slowly, Jessica walked to the end of the board. She knew that when she dove there would be no way to judge how soon she would hit the water. She would meet its cold surface without warning. She paused.

"Two ways down, Jessica," Bruce called. "You can always go back down the ladder."

"No way," Jessica called out.

Then, she quickly raised her arms over her head, and dove out into the darkness.

Almost immediately, she hit the water and plunged down deep. By instinct, Jessica bent her body upward and kicked. In a moment, she reached the surface of the water. Then she climbed out of the pool.

Jessica stood dripping by the edge of the pool. She felt a satisfying surge of success. Now she knew she could create the danger and control the fear. At that moment she felt that there was nothing she couldn't do.

"Bruce, you should never, never, never underestimate me," she called out to where he stood in the dark.

The SWEET VALLEY HIGH series, published by Bantam Books. Ask your bookseller for any titles you have missed.

SWEET VALLEY High.

JESSICA AGAINST BRUCE

Written by
Kate William

Created by
FRANCINE PASCAL

BANTAM BOOKS
NEW YORK · TORONTO · LONDON · SYDNEY · AUCKLAND

JESSICA AGAINST BRUCE
A BANTAM BOOK 0 553 29232 3

Originally published in USA by Bantam Books

First publication in Great Britain

PRINTING HISTORY
Bantam edition published 1992
Reprinted 1994
TV tie-in edition published 1995

The trademarks "Sweet Valley" and "Sweet Valley High"
are owned by Francine Pascal and are used under license by
Bantam Books and Transworld Publishers Ltd.

Conceived by Francine Pascal

Produced by Daniel Weiss Associates, Inc.,
33 West 17th Street, New York, New York 10011

Bantam Books are published by Transworld Publishers Ltd,
61–63 Uxbridge Road, Ealing, London W5 5SA,
in Australia by Transworld Publishers (Australia) Pty Ltd,
15–25 Helles Avenue, Moorebank, NSW 2170,
and in New Zealand by Transworld Publishers (NZ) Ltd,
3 William Pickering Drive, Albany, Auckland.

Printed and bound in Great Britain by
Cox & Wyman Ltd, Reading, Berkshire.

One

"If I had known we were having an assembly, I would have brought a magazine to school," Jessica Wakefield said as she slumped into a seat in the auditorium. Members of the student body of Sweet Valley High were busily trying to find seats, and the sounds of a hundred conversations filled the air.

"I thought you did all your magazine reading during math," teased Jessica's identical twin, Elizabeth.

"Oh, no, I do my nails during math," Jessica replied with a sarcastic smile.

Elizabeth grinned. Her sister had never won any prizes for academic diligence. That just wasn't her style. Of course, she did win honors and distinctions of other kinds. Jessica's reputation as one of Sweet Valley High's most fun, most adventurous, and most spontaneous juniors was built on a solid foundation. The latest dance craze, the hottest albums, the trendiest clothes—Jessica was always in on the ground floor. Recently, when the twins had landed a week's stint on a soap opera in Los Angeles, nobody was surprised that Jessica had jumped into the Hollywood party scene.

Elizabeth knew that people were amazed that she and Jessica were twin sisters. It would be hard to imagine a greater contrast between two people. Elizabeth *did* win academic awards, and her reputation was built on hard work, loyalty, and fairness. Her friends counted on her as the person who always listened sympathetically and tried not to pass judgment. Her favorite way to spend time was reading or writing, or else being with her steady boyfriend, Todd Wilkins.

Yet these extremes of personality did not keep Elizabeth and Jessica from being best friends. They clashed often, but there was a special bond between them that always brought them back together. Covering for each other and helping each other through tight spots were top priorities for both of them. Sometimes that even meant trading identities. It was easy for either twin to pass herself off as the other. Both had sun-streaked blond hair and eyes the color of the nearby Pacific Ocean, perfect size-six figures, and lovely, heart-shaped faces.

"When is this thing going to get started?" Jessica complained with a dramatic groan.

"Would you rather be in French class?" asked Elizabeth's best friend, Enid Rollins.

2

As the bickering went on, Mr. Cooper, Sweet Valley High's principal, walked onto the stage and blew into the microphone. "Testing, testing, is this thing on?" he asked. The microphone let out a piercing whine of feedback, and everyone yelled, "It's on!"

"OK, settle down, people," Mr. Cooper said. "I have an extremely important announcement to make."

"It's always extremely important," Jessica muttered.

"Shh," Elizabeth said, nudging Jessica with her elbow.

"We have been chosen for a very special honor," the principal continued. "The International Federation of Teachers is sending a delegation of guest observers to several schools in California. For the next three Thursdays, these guest teachers will be visiting our school."

"Wow," Elizabeth said. "This'll be great!"

"I'm trembling with excitement," Jessica whispered. Elizabeth rolled her eyes.

"The teachers represent countries all over the world," Mr. Cooper explained. "England, France, India, Russia—" He broke off to glance at some papers in front of him. "I want to impress on each and every one of you what an honor this is for Sweet Valley High. And I expect you all to be on your very best behavior during their visits."

"No dancing on the cafeteria tables," Jessica said, leaning over the seats.

"Do we have to salute?" Lila whispered loudly.

"This sounds like a big yawn," Jessica said. She

3

demonstrated her prediction with an ostentatious yawn, patting her open mouth with her hand.

"Also at this time," Mr. Cooper continued, "I will be inviting a select group of students to be part of our host committee."

"Guess who'll get picked," Enid said in Elizabeth's ear. "You."

Elizabeth smiled. In spite of Jessica and Lila's obligatory scorn for the project, she thought it sounded interesting. She hoped she *would* have a chance to meet some of the visiting teachers and find out what high schools in other countries were like.

"So in conclusion," Mr. Cooper said, "I want to repeat my request that you show our guests what a terrific, top-notch school we have here. And I thank you ahead of time for your cooperation."

As the principal left the podium, everyone began to rise and file out. "Don't forget to demonstrate your very best behavior," Lila reminded Jessica.

Elizabeth looked at the ceiling and sighed. As far as Jessica was concerned, a request for good behavior was like a red flag to a bull: an invitation for trouble.

At four o'clock that afternoon, Jessica was surrounded by a crowd of friends in a booth at the Dairi Burger. She listened to the chatter that flowed around her and quietly sipped her diet soda.

4

"I hope these visiting teachers aren't going to ask us a bunch of dumb questions," Amy Sutton said.

Lila fingered one of the gold bracelets on her wrist and shook her head. "Come on, Amy. They're teachers. Teachers are born to ask dumb questions."

Everyone laughed. Jessica smiled and looked down into her drink. Though she shared her friends' feelings about teachers in general, she was feeling slightly melancholy and not in the mood for joking. Her steady boyfriend, Sam Woodruff, had left for Colorado to attend a special program at the state university. Sam had applied for and had been accepted to a course for high school seniors thinking of making a career of environmental science. He would be gone for nearly a month. Jessica missed him so much it hurt. It made her miserable to think of not seeing him for such a long time, particularly since they had just made up after a huge fight.

Actually, the fight had been all her fault. Landing a cameo role on *The Young and the Beautiful*, her favorite soap opera, had taken more than her usual amount of scheming. Elizabeth, in one of her rare stubborn moods, had refused to audition at first. But her sister's refusal hadn't defeated Jessica. Part of her determination had to do with her serious crush on Brandon Hunter, the drop-dead-handsome star of the show. For one dreamlike, whirlwind week, Brandon had squired Jessica to various Hollywood openings and parties, and their pictures had been splashed all over the gos-

5

sip pages. Headlines speculating about Brandon Hunter's "adorable new love" had hit Sam pretty hard, and Jessica had been too star-struck to be sympathetic to his feelings.

When Jessica finally found out that Brandon had only been using her to create a publicity blitz, she used a live broadcast of the soap opera to tell Brandon off and to make up with Sam at the same time. She was more in love with Sam now than ever, and it was doubly depressing that he was gone.

"What's wrong with Jessica?" Amy asked loudly.

Everyone at their table turned to stare. Jessica's cheeks colored. She didn't want to admit she was moping over her boyfriend.

"I'm just so bored," she explained quickly.

Aaron Dallas leaned over the back of the seat from the next booth. "Jessica, you're not boring."

"I said bored, not boring," Jessica replied, refusing to rise to the bait.

"Wakefield's right," Bruce Patman announced to the place at large. "It *is* boring around here." Bruce made this declaration in his usual tone of extreme superiority. Being a senior wasn't the only thing that made Bruce Patman think he was God's gift to America. He was also very rich and a natural-born snob—the license plate on his black Porsche read "1BRUCE1." Recently, Bruce had been intimating that he had already done everything there was to do in Sweet Valley, and that he was craving excitement and stimulation.

"No one around here ever tries to break the

6

mold," he went on with an irritable look marking his handsome features. "Not one single person in this entire place has a sense of adventure. If any of you were put in a dangerous situation you'd probably just curl up and die."

"Why don't *you* just curl up and die, Bruce," Lila snapped at him.

"Yeah," Jessica agreed. "Put up or shut up. You're always complaining about how dull Sweet Valley is, but you never do anything about it."

Amy laughed. "That's right, Patman. You're just blowing more hot air."

Aaron and Ken each burst out laughing at the furious expression on Bruce's face. "He's been talking like this for days," Ken said to the girls. "He's beginning to sound like a broken record."

"Broken record—broken record—broken record," intoned Barry Rork, Amy's boyfriend and one of Bruce's tennis teammates.

"I knew it," Bruce said, sneering. "I knew you all would be too scared to admit you need some danger in your lives. You're like a bunch of middle-aged bankers."

Jessica ripped the end off a straw wrapper, turned around, and blew the paper off the straw into Bruce's face. He swatted it away. "How's that for danger?" she asked sweetly.

She gazed at him and batted her eyelashes, enjoying the flush of anger that swept across Bruce's cheeks. There had been a time when she thought they would make the perfect couple, but before long she had realized they were like pickles and ice cream—totally incompatible.

7

Bruce stood up and stalked out of the Dairi Burger. At the doorway he bumped into Elizabeth. He scowled at her, too, then slammed the door behind him.

"What a joke," Jessica muttered.

"What's going on?" Elizabeth asked, joining her sister at the booth. "Bruce's face looked like a thunder cloud."

Lila chuckled. "The usual—we're all hopelessly boring and conservative and Bruce is fed up with every one of us."

"Bruce wants *danger*," Jessica explained with a grin. "Maybe he'll get lucky and someone will try to run him down with a car."

"If Bruce wants danger and excitement, I'm sure he'll be able to find some," Elizabeth said.

"Or buy some," Barry suggested.

"Well I, for one, hope he gets his wish," Jessica announced, rattling the ice in her cup. "Then maybe that irritating whining sound I always hear when he's around will go away."

Elizabeth and Jessica drove to school the next day in their new Jeep with Elizabeth at the wheel. The twins had finally talked their parents into helping them buy a new vehicle since their old Fiat convertible had kept breaking down. Elizabeth had done most of the negotiating with the dealer, and whenever she sat at the wheel of the black and chrome Jeep she felt a certain pride.

"You know," Elizabeth began as she pulled into a parking space, "I shouldn't admit this to you, but I'm hoping Mr. Cooper asks me to be on the committee to host the visiting teachers."

"I'm totally shocked and surprised, Liz," Jessica said.

Elizabeth opened her door and got out. "I just think it would be interesting to meet the teachers. You don't want him to ask *you*, do you?" she added.

"Oh, I see, you're doing me a favor." Jessica swung her book bag over her shoulder. "Thank you for saving me from a fate worse than death."

Elizabeth grinned at her twin. Side by side, they walked toward Sweet Valley High. Up ahead, they saw a tall, familiar figure swaggering in the same direction.

"The dreaded Bruce," Jessica groaned. Then she narrowed her eyes. "What's that he's wearing?"

Elizabeth looked ahead. Bruce was wearing a black leather jacket, and emblazoned across the back was a large X.

"What does *that* mean?" Elizabeth wondered.

"I hope it's a target," Jessica said. She held up her hand, squinted along one finger, and pretended to aim.

A group of boys had now congregated around Bruce, and Elizabeth and Jessica had to pass them to get into the building.

"Hey, Wakefield," Bruce called out as they walked by.

Elizabeth and Jessica both stopped and looked toward him without speaking. Elizabeth was always aggravated by his cocky, arrogant manner.

"I decided to take your advice, Jessica," Bruce went on, giving her a lazy grin.

Jessica put both hands to her heart. "Oh, I'm so flattered," she gasped. "I actually said something worth listening to?"

Some of the boys gathered around Bruce laughed. Conversations between Jessica and Bruce usually ended up as sparring matches. Although it was sometimes fun to watch, Elizabeth wished her sister wouldn't encourage him at all. Right now, she would prefer simply to walk away from him.

"That's right, Wakefield," Bruce went on, ignoring Jessica's sarcasm. "I've started my own club—for real men."

"*Real* men?" Elizabeth blurted, unable to resist Bruce's last remark. "And just what is *that* supposed to mean?"

"Real men who know real excitement when they see it," Bruce explained.

Jessica burst out laughing. "Do you have a secret handshake?"

"Very funny," Bruce said, turning away.

The white X embroidered on the back of his leather jacket gleamed in the sunlight. Elizabeth was sure he wanted them to ask what it was all about, but she didn't think she had the stomach for it.

"Come on," she said to Jessica. "Let's go."

As Jessica fell into step beside her, Elizabeth shook her head. "He never ceases to amaze me. You'd think belonging to Phi Epsilon would be enough for him," Elizabeth said, referring to the popular fraternity of which her boyfriend, Todd Wilkins, was also a member. "He sure made a big enough deal over the last rushes."

"Real men," Jessica muttered. "Give me a break. This must be the stupidest thing Bruce has ever come up with—and he's come up with some *pretty* stupid things."

Elizabeth nodded. She didn't particularly care what Bruce was up to this time, but she had a feeling that they were all going to hear more about it, whether they wanted to or not.

Two

Jessica sat at her usual table in the cafeteria the next day at lunchtime. Lila, Amy, and Rosa Jameson were already there, along with Maria Santelli and Jean West. Jessica reached across the table and helped herself to one of Lila's french fries.

"Mind if I mooch?" she asked as she delicately nipped off the end of it.

Lila shrugged. "Mooch away."

Jessica glanced around the cafeteria. Much as she hated to admit it, Bruce was right about Sweet Valley being boring. It wasn't such a bad place, she realized, but nothing was *new* anymore. She had enough sense to know that part of her grumpiness was due to Sam's absence, and to the relatively quiet pace her life had returned to after the hectic days of the soap opera but she still wished there would be a little shake-up of some

12

kind. *Just a little excitement,* she thought. *Something to stir things up a bit.*

Briefly, her imagination ran over the way things might have been. The producers of *The Young and the Beautiful* had offered her and Elizabeth the chance to continue their roles on the show, but they had both decided against it. Though at the time she had been firm in her decision, Jessica now wondered if it wouldn't have been smarter to have accepted the offer. She had wanted to spend more time with Sam, but now he was away, and she didn't have anything to do.

"Hey," Lila said, breaking into Jessica's day-dreaming. "Look at that."

They all looked toward the cafeteria door. Bruce had just walked in, wearing his new "X" jacket, and Ronnie Edwards was at his side. Ronnie turned to speak to someone behind him, and everyone at Jessica's table saw that he wore a jacket identical to Bruce's.

"What is the deal with this Club X thing, anyway?" Amy asked in a petulant tone. "Bruce got all mysterious when I asked him yesterday. He said it's for men only."

"I didn't know Ronnie Edwards qualified," Lila drawled.

"Why not ask Barry to find out?" Jean suggested. "Isn't he curious, too?"

Amy rolled her eyes. "Yeah, but he'll say that if he asks and Bruce makes him promise not to tell, he'll have to keep the promise. It's one of those male-bonding things. Typical."

Jessica frowned as a group of guys converged

on Bruce and Ronnie. From their eager, questioning looks and gestures, she could tell they were all asking about Club X. It seemed that Bruce and Ronnie were the only members; it also seemed that there were plenty of guys who *wanted* to be members.

"Hey, girls," Bruce said airily as he passed by their table, surrounded by several other guys.

"Come on, Bruce," Rosa said with a smile. "You've got us interested. What's your club all about?"

Ronnie squared his shoulders inside his leather jacket. "Sorry, Rosa. Guys only."

"It sounds like the Elks Club or something," Lila said to the girls. "Totally thrilling."

"Or the Boy Scouts," Jean added, her eyes twinkling.

Jessica laughed. "I bet they play with GI Joes in Bruce's backyard."

"Bruce gets to be the general, and the other guys have to be grunts," Rosa said. She saluted smartly. "Yes, sir! No, sir! Yes, your mighty generalship, sir!"

"So, Bruce," Jessica said, meeting his eyes defiantly. "When are you going to let girls join?"

"No fair making it boys only," Amy chimed in. "What about equal rights and all of that?"

Bruce looked at Ronnie, and they both smiled tolerantly. "Girls just don't have what it takes," Bruce explained in his most patronizing tone. "It's just a fact of nature."

"What exactly does it *take*?" Jessica snapped. "A big mouth?"

The girls at her table laughed. Jessica felt her cheeks flush with the thrill of battle.

"Come on, Bruce," Jessica persisted. "They even let women join the army, you know."

Bruce sent the other boys a grin. "I think Sam should hurry up and get back to Sweet Valley so he can keep Jessica in line."

Some of the guys cheered and Bruce folded his arms across his chest.

"You are the biggest sexist pig in this school, Bruce Patman," Rosa said. "No, scratch that. You're the biggest sexist pig in California."

"I bet I can do whatever it is a person has to do to join your stupid club," Jessica declared, standing up and placing her hands on her hips.

A smile curled Bruce's lips, and his blue eyes sparkled maliciously. "I know, you just want to spend more time with me to rekindle those old flames of passion."

"Whooa!" Aaron Dallas said. "Stand back—she's gonna blow!"

Jessica swallowed her fury. True, she and Bruce had dated for a little while—but it was ancient history, now. They were both much too head-strong to be able to get along in a relationship. A relationship meant compromise, and compromise with Bruce was one thing she had never been able to achieve. Ever since, it had been open war between them.

Still, Jessica couldn't deny that there was a powerful spark between them. He was sexy and provocative, and Jessica could never resist rising to his bait. She knew there was nothing romantic

15

about it at all, nothing that should make Sam jealous. It was more like an old ritual between them, a running contest to see who could score most often and hit the hardest. For the moment, Bruce had won, and Jessica was seething.

"You're not going to let him get away with that, are you, Jess?" Lila prodded.

"Get away with what?" Jessica said sweetly. "I don't consider Bruce's lies or his dumb, sexist comments much of a threat. They're the mark of a small mind."

Ken let out a howl of laughter, and slapped Bruce on the back. "Ouch," he said. "That one was a killer, Bruce. She got you good."

"Anyway, as I was saying," Bruce cut in, ignoring Ken's comment and turning his back on Jessica and her friends, "it's a club only guys have the guts to handle. If any of you are interested, though, I'll be sitting over there."

With one last arrogant smile over his shoulder, Bruce sauntered away with Ronnie swaggering at his side.

"Bruce is all talk," Jessica said, sitting down again and leaning her elbows on the table. "Whatever the club involves is probably a lot less outrageous than he'd like everyone to think."

"That crack about only guys having the guts to take it really burns me up, too," Amy said.

Jessica nodded. "I think we should all try to get in, just to prove to Bruce—and everyone else—what a jerk he really is."

"I agree," Lila said. "I hate it when Bruce lords it over people—particularly me."

"OK, so you're all with me, right?" Jessica said.

Rosa, Jean, and Maria looked at her doubtfully. "I really don't want to get wrapped up in this club," Maria said. "With Bruce and Ronnie as members, it probably just means trouble."

"I'm out, too," Rosa said, shaking her head. "I think it's great that you're sticking up for equal rights, Jess, but I've got enough to handle right now with schoolwork and all."

Jean just held up both hands. "And you can count me out, too," she said.

"You two, then," Jessica said, turning back to Lila and Amy. "We'll show them."

"Right," Amy said with a firm nod.

Lila folded her arms across her chest. "If it'll bring Bruce down, I'm in."

"Great," Jessica said determinedly. "We'll show them all!"

Elizabeth and Todd were deep in conversation when Mr. Collins, their English teacher, interrupted.

"Messages from our leader," he said, waving two identical pink slips of paper.

Elizabeth read her note aloud: "Please come to Mr. Cooper's office at seventh period."

"We've been summoned, Mr. Collins," Elizabeth said apologetically. "Are you going to assign homework?"

Mr. Collins waved them out. "Just read to the end of *Silas Marner*," he said with a smile.

"What did we do?" Todd wondered out loud, as

17

they hurried down the hall to the principal's office. "I haven't committed any major crimes today."

"None that you know of," Elizabeth teased him.

When they arrived at the office, one of the secretaries ushered them into Mr. Cooper's inner office. Enid was already there, as well as Penny Ayala, Bill Chase, and Dan Scott.

"We're all busted," Dan quipped. "I told them I didn't do it, whatever it was."

"What's going on?" Elizabeth asked, taking a seat next to Enid.

Enid looked as puzzled as the others. "I don't know."

"Well, here you all are," said Mr. Cooper, walking in and closing the door. "Good, then let's get started."

As he sat behind his desk, Elizabeth felt a sudden jolt of adrenaline. It hadn't occurred to her until that moment, but she was sure they had all been chosen to host the visiting teachers. She sat forward in her chair and smiled.

"Now," the principal said as he ran one hand over his bald head, "you all know about the International Teachers' Project, and you know I want some of our best and brightest students to represent Sweet Valley High and to host our guests. Well, you've been chosen."

"Cool," Dan said.

"What sort of responsibilities will we have, Mr. Cooper?" Todd asked.

"Well," Mr. Cooper said, "on the days the teachers spend with us, you'll each be excused

18

from a half day of classes, either morning or afternoon. You'll be divided into two teams, and it will be your responsibility to take our guests around the school and to answer any questions they might have."

"Is there a specific schedule we'll be following?" Enid asked.

"Yes," Mr. Cooper answered, giving her a quick smile. "I want the teachers to see as much as possible. You might even find yourselves taking them to your own classes. I also want them to see all of our facilities—gymnasium, theater, art studios . . ."

"The cafeteria?" Penny supplied.

"Most definitely," Mr. Cooper agreed. "I hardly need to say that our cafeteria staff will be on full alert, and I think we can expect some pretty tasty lunches."

"Mr. Cooper?" Elizabeth asked. "Will we be allowed to ask the teachers questions about their own countries, or wouldn't that be polite?"

Mr. Cooper sat back in his chair and beamed at her. "Of course you can ask questions. That's why I picked you, Elizabeth. You're intelligent, responsible—"

"Miss Perfect," Todd whispered.

As subtly as she could, Elizabeth dug her elbow sharply into Todd's ribs, smiling innocently at Mr. Cooper the whole time.

"Yes," Mr. Cooper finished, "by all means, ask our guests questions. This project is supposed to be an exchange of ideas," he said, meshing his fingers to demonstrate his point.

19

"The teachers are coming tomorrow, aren't they?" Bill asked.

"Yes. These are your schedules for tomorrow," Mr. Cooper said, passing each of them a sheet of paper. "Enid, Penny, and Dan, you're the morning team. Elizabeth, Todd, and Bill, you've got afternoon duty. Your teachers will excuse you from your classes. Meet me here after homeroom, team one, and at the beginning of fifth period, team two. Got it?"

As they filed out, Penny spoke in a low voice behind Elizabeth and Todd. "Do you think we should all synchronize our watches?"

Todd glanced back with a grin. "I never could figure out that military time stuff—eighteen hundred hours, twenty-one hundred hours. I'd be a total failure."

"Seriously, isn't this great?" Elizabeth said enthusiastically.

"Yeah. And we get out of classes, too," Todd answered.

Elizabeth laughed. She could tell that Todd was looking forward to their new job as much as she was.

At dinner that night, Elizabeth told her family, including her older brother, Steven, who was home from college on a short break, about being chosen to show the visiting teachers around.

"I think that sounds terrific, Liz," Mrs. Wakefield said proudly.

Mr. Wakefield helped himself to some salad.

"Just remember one thing, Liz," he said. "Some of the teachers will have very different ideas and ways of doing things. Try to be tactful."

"Ned!" Mrs. Wakefield laughed. "You're talking to Miss Tactful USA."

Mr. Wakefield shrugged and winked at Elizabeth. "You know what I mean, Liz. Some of them might have old-fashioned ideas about discipline or gender roles. That sort of thing."

"Like maybe one of them will say that girls shouldn't play sports," Jessica suggested. "To be honest, I for one wouldn't mind if girls didn't have to take gym class. I hate getting hot and sweaty in the middle of the day!"

"I'll be very discreet, I promise," Elizabeth said with a smile for her father. "I won't argue about anything. Unless it's *really* serious," she added.

Jessica hooked one leg underneath her and sat on her foot so she could reach across the table for the salt. "*Speaking* of gender roles . . ." she began in her most gossipy voice.

"Pass the pepper, please," Steven said through a mouthful of food.

"Liz, do you have any white clothes that need washing tonight?" Mrs. Wakefield asked politely.

"No, I did some laundry yesterday," Elizabeth said, trying not to smile while the family pretended they hadn't heard Jessica. It was a family joke to tease Jessica when she had particularly juicy news she was eager to spread around.

Typically, Jessica ignored the fact that they were pretending to ignore her. "Bruce started some hotshot club," she explained, shaking salt on her

21

carrot sticks. "And he says it's for men only. Like he's really a *man!*"

"OK, I'll bite, Jess," Mrs. Wakefield said, smiling. "Are you planning to crash the gates of sex discrimination?"

"I thought Liz was the feminist around here," Steven put in. "You fell for that beauty-pageant stuff hook, line, and sinker, Jess."

Not long ago, Jessica had defended her right to enter the Miss Teen Sweet Valley competition. If there was one thing that Elizabeth couldn't stand, it was contests in which the only thing that mattered was a good figure and a pretty smile. In fact, her chief objection to auditioning for the soap opera was that the women characters on the show were either empty-headed bimbos or scheming witches. Stereotyping in beauty pageants and on the soaps were equally revolting to her.

"Totally different situation," Jessica declared with a toss of her head. "Somebody has to prove to Bruce and his entourage that girls can do anything boys can do. We're just as smart, we have more endurance, we're probably *more* creative, *and* we're equally as brave. In fact, in everything *I* can think of, women are at *least* equal to men."

Elizabeth nodded. "Well, I agree with you there, Jess. But why would you want to join a club *Bruce* started?"

"That's not the point, Liz," Jessica insisted.

"I just don't understand why you feel you have to prove yourself to him, of all people," Elizabeth persisted.

Jessica sighed patiently. "I'm not proving *myself*

22

to him," she said. "I'm proving a *point* to him. And to all the other guys who think Bruce is right. They're saying that guys are stronger, smarter, braver, tougher—you name it, according to them guys can do it better."

"I know plenty of guys like that at college," Steven said. "Their line is that it's just a fact of nature that there are some things females can't do—because they're females."

Mrs. Wakefield let out an indignant breath. "I'd like them to see Liz change the oil and air filter in the Jeep!"

"And *I* wish they could have seen her negotiate the commission right out from under that car salesman!" Mr. Wakefield added.

"Problem is, you can't argue with that kind of guy," Steven went on regretfully. "They have to see something with their own eyes, and even then, they'll try to argue that it was just a fluke or beginner's luck or something like that."

"I have to say, I agree with Jessica about wanting to join this club," Mr. Wakefield said after a moment's pause.

Elizabeth looked at her father in surprise. "You do?"

"Sure," he said with a nod. "Steven's right, too. Some men just don't get the point unless you hit them over the head with it."

Jessica let out a high-spirited laugh. "And I can't wait to do just that to Bruce!"

23

Three

Jessica took her seat in first period French the following day, wearily opened her French book, and prepared to be bored. Ms. Dalton was infuriatingly persistent about pronunciation, and she sometimes drilled a single student on one sentence for what seemed like five minutes at a time.

"Did you do the homework?" Lila asked her, sitting down at the next desk.

"Why? Didn't—" Jessica began. As she spoke, the fire alarms all over the school began to clang.

"Fire drill," Lila moaned. "I just sat down!"

"All right, class," Ms. Dalton said, taking her purse from her bottom desk-drawer. "Single file. You know the procedure."

The bells were clamoring so loudly that Jessica had to cover her ears as they went into the hall. All up and down the corridor, doors were opening and students and teachers were streaming out to the exits. Jessica and the rest of the French class went outside to the front lawn.

"Perfect timing," Lila said, sitting down on the grass. "My French homework for today was not exactly a *fait accompli*."

"Well *mine* was," Jessica said huffily. It was irritating that on one of the rare days that her homework was done, there was a fire drill during class. "It's not fair."

"Hi," Elizabeth said as she walked up with Todd.

"Take a seat," Jessica invited.

Jessica was watching Ms. Dalton and Mrs. Ray, the Spanish teacher. They both looked puzzled and exasperated, and Mrs. Ray kept shaking her head. Jessica stood up.

"I'll be right back," Jessica said, walking toward the two teachers and keeping her ears open.

"Nobody told me there was a drill scheduled," Ms. Dalton was saying. "I had a lot to get done this period, and this is going to throw my schedule off."

"Mr. Cooper *promised* to warn us ahead of time," Mrs. Ray complained.

Jessica strolled back to the others and sat down on the ground.

"Unscheduled fire drill," she announced. "The teachers didn't know about it."

Elizabeth looked quickly at the school. "You don't think there could be a real fire, do you?" she asked anxiously.

"Wouldn't that be heaven?" Lila asked dreamily. "No more school."

25

Fire sirens could be heard approaching from a distance. Jessica lay back on the grass, ready to take full advantage of the unexpected free period to work on her tan.

"This looks really serious," Elizabeth murmured nervously as the fire trucks pulled up in front of the school.

Jessica raised herself up on one elbow. There wasn't a trace of smoke anywhere near the brick building, and she was sure that the fire fighters would be gone in a minute. It looked very much like a false alarm.

And then Jessica wondered if someone had triggered it on purpose. Perhaps someone with a killer test or someone trying to escape an oral report had pulled the fire alarm to get out of class. There had been plenty of "unscheduled drills" in the past that had eventually been traced back to a student. Jessica had even considered pulling a false alarm herself once or twice, although she knew she would never be crazy enough to go through with it.

As her eyes wandered over the crowded lawn, she caught sight of something that was becoming all too familiar: a black jacket embroidered with a glaring white X. The person wearing the jacket was a surprise to her, though.

"Take a look," she said, nodding her head in that direction. "Tad Johnson's in Bruce's club."

"Tad?" Lila echoed, turning around. "He's not one of Bruce's friends."

"I know," Jessica said, frowning hard.

Tad Johnson was hardly Bruce's type. Conser-

26

vative guesses put his weight at about two hundred and forty pounds, and as far as Jessica knew, Tad's only interests in life were playing football and watching football. He didn't exactly fit in with Bruce's cool-as-ice image.

"So what *is* it the guys have to do to get in?" Jessica said in a frustrated tone. "Obviously it doesn't matter if you're one of Bruce's friends."

Lila raised an eyebrow. "I'm amazed they could even find a leather jacket in Tad's size."

Tad, Bruce, and Ronnie were leaning against a tree, hands in their jacket pockets and grins of superiority on their faces. While Jessica watched, Ronnie held one hand up in the air and Tad slapped it, laughing.

"Look at them," Jessica fumed. "The three of them are acting like they just won the lottery, or pulled off the insider-trading deal of the century."

Stretching out one leg to admire her tan, Lila let out a short laugh. "Maybe one of them pulled the fire alarm," she suggested.

"Yeah, sure," Jessica scoffed. But then her smile faded. Deep in thought, Jessica lay back again and closed her eyes against the sun, waiting for the signal to return to class. Maybe they *were* responsible, after all.

At lunchtime, Jessica arrived at her usual cafeteria table in the middle of heated speculation about Club X.

"I heard there's some kind of initiation thing," Amy said, her light blue eyes gleaming.

27

"Yeah, I heard it was some kind of macho test," Denise Hadley contributed.

Jessica threw herself into a chair. "Oh, please! Do we have to talk about Club X all the time?" she demanded loudly. "I wish it were Club Explode and they'd all disappear in a puff of smoke."

"Kind of makes things interesting, though, doesn't it?" Bruce asked, sitting down next to her with a big grin on his handsome face.

"Just fascinating, Bruce," Jessica shot back.

His smile widened. "Maybe you girls can start a fan club," Bruce suggested. "Wear your shortest skirts, OK? I like that."

"You're so obnoxious," Jessica said, curling her lip.

"You can cheer us on from the sidelines," Bruce continued smugly, giving his friends a cocky smile.

"I bet Jessica can pass any initiation test you have," Maria said.

Jessica narrowed her eyes at Bruce. "But try to think of something more original than another fire drill."

Bruce chuckled. "Jessica, Jessica, Jessica. You have such an imagination," he said, patronizing her as usual.

"Jessica wouldn't do something stupid like that," Sandy said. "But she *could* if she wanted to."

"Right, Bruce," Denise said. "Jessica can do anything she sets her mind to do."

"Girls can do *anything* boys can do," Amy insisted. "There are women at the top of every single profession. Like Justice Sandra Day O'Connor, for example."

"Or Susan Butcher," Terri Adams said. "She's won the Iditarod, that incredible dog-sled race in Alaska, *several* times."

"Want any more examples?" Jessica asked sarcastically.

Bruce leaned back in his chair and appealed to the guys at the next table. "Did you hear that? Girls can do anything guys can do."

"Yeah, sure," Ken said with a laugh. "I'd like to see one of them run a touchdown pass through Palisades High's defensive line."

Terri hooted. "You know perfectly well that Claire Middleton is as good a quarterback as you are, Ken."

"Oh, well . . . that's different," Ken mumbled, staring down at his sandwich. Terri was the football team's assistant manager, as well as Ken's girlfriend. Jessica hoped Terri wouldn't let Ken off too easily for that crack!

Jessica grinned. She was glad that her friends were beginning to get into the spirit of the fight. It struck her as ironic, too, that Bruce's decision to make things more lively at Sweet Valley High was actually working. It wasn't every day that there was a huge, juicy debate to get involved in.

"Here's another example. Can you think of anything braver than going into space?" Denise demanded. "Sally Ride has done it."

Bruce shrugged. "There are always exceptions to the rule."

29

"Yeah. No way could any of *you* girls get into Club X," Ronnie announced. He tipped his chair back. "No way in a million years."

"We *could* if we *wanted* to," Maria insisted. "But who wants to?"

"Jessica does," Lila said.

Jessica glanced quickly at her friend. "And so do Lila and Amy. Just to shut you up once and for all, and to show that girls are just as brave and smart and capable as any of you guys. Even *more* than you guys, in fact."

"In your dreams, Wakefield," Bruce said.

"You're the one living in a dream," Jean retorted. "The only thing girls can't do is become fathers. Is *that* what you have to do to join?" she demanded with a triumphant smile at the other girls.

Ronnie was shaking his head emphatically. "I don't care what you say, women are not equal to men. Women are in the military, but they can't be put in combat. No woman in the world can carry an eighty-pound pack, plus weapons, and crawl through the mud to kill the enemy."

"Oh, really?" Sandy Bacon said. "My cousin Allison is in the army, and I bet she could run *you* right into the ground."

"Sorry," Bruce insisted, raising his voice in a lordly manner. "You can't convince me that any girl or woman faced with danger won't cry for help."

"*What?*" several girls shouted in outrage.

As the argument escalated around her, Jessica took a slip of paper and scribbled a note on it.

"Here, Bruce," she said, raising her voice over the din.

He took it and arched one eyebrow. "What is this?" he asked.

Jessica gave him her sweetest smile. "My jacket size," she said. "Make sure the X is *really* big. I want everyone to see it."

"Way to go, Jess," Terri applauded.

Bruce narrowed his eyes at Jessica. Then he chuckled. "Be careful, Jess. You just might get what you wish for."

Elizabeth hurried to the administration office at the beginning of fifth period. Todd and Bill were already there, talking with Mr. Cooper and the delegation of visiting teachers.

"Hi," she said breathlessly as she joined them. "Sorry I'm late."

"This is the third member of your afternoon tour-guide group," Mr. Cooper said in his hearty voice to the assembled teachers. He put one hand on Elizabeth's shoulder. "Elizabeth Wakefield. She's one of our best students."

Elizabeth turned to meet the guests with a friendly smile. "How do you do?"

One by one, the teachers introduced themselves. They were Mr. Turner-Cox, of Great Britain; Madame Erlane, of France; Mr. Srinivasen, of India; Mrs. Ochiba, of Japan; and Mrs. Vlasaya, of Russia. Fortunately, each teacher wore a name tag with his or her home country's flag printed on it. Elizabeth's head was already spinning with the unfamiliar names.

"We're enjoying ourselves immensely," Mr. Turner-Cox, the delegate from England, said in what Elizabeth thought must be an Oxford accent.

"Your school is very nice," Madame Erlane added.

"*Bienvenue à* Sweet Valley High," Elizabeth said to the teacher from France.

Mr. Cooper nodded and smiled and rubbed his hands together. "Wonderful. Well, kids. They're all yours. Your first stop is the cafeteria. Enjoy your lunch."

"It's this way," Todd said, ushering the teachers ahead of him.

On the way to the lunchroom, Elizabeth fell into step beside Mr. Srinivasen, the teacher from India. His lilting accent was so melodious that Elizabeth found herself listening to the sound of his voice rather than to his actual words. She came to herself with a start when he asked her a question.

"Are you in the college preparatory program?" he asked.

Elizabeth shook her head. "Sweet Valley High is not really set up like that," she explained. "Our public schools are for everyone, regardless of plans to go on to college."

"But you will attend university, yourself?" he continued with a polite smile.

"Definitely," Elizabeth said. "I think most of the students here will go on to college. We have pretty high academic standards."

As she spoke, she opened the cafeteria door. Instantly, a wave of noise engulfed them. Elizabeth, Todd, and Bill halted in their tracks, their visitors grouped behind them.

Inside the lunchroom some kind of a riot seemed to be going on. Near the center of the room, a crowd of people were standing between several tables, waving their hands and shouting at the tops of their lungs.

"What is going on?" Mr. Turner-Cox asked in astonishment.

Elizabeth felt her cheeks flush. "I—I'm not sure," she stammered. She shot Todd a questioning glance, but he looked as baffled as she felt.

"Has there been an accident?" asked Mr. Srinivasen.

"Equal rights for women!" somebody in the crowd shouted.

"Men and women are not the same, and you know it!" someone else yelled.

"Women want to call themselves nurturers," one boy insisted loudly. "And then they turn around and say they want someone else to watch their kids while they go to work!"

The teacher from Japan, Mrs. Ochiba, looked scandalized. "This does not happen in our schools!" she said.

"What's going on?" Elizabeth asked Todd and Bill in a low voice.

At that moment, the crowd shifted and Elizabeth saw her twin sister in the center of the hurricane, shouting at Bruce. "Oh, no," Elizabeth groaned.

"It's just a discussion about equality between men and women," Bill said, turning to the teachers with a slightly nervous smile.

"Probably continuing a discussion from social studies class," Todd added weakly.

The visiting teachers took in the scene with varying degrees of surprise and disapproval. Finally, Mr. Turner-Cox let out a laugh. "You Yanks," he said. "You're so outspoken."

"This is a *debate*?" Madame Erlane asked doubtfully.

"That's right, a debate," Elizabeth said quickly. "Our teachers encourage us to think about classroom questions outside of class. Some of us take that pretty seriously, as you can see."

Naturally, Elizabeth had no desire to explain what she supposed was the origin of the so-called debate—that Jessica had probably been goading Bruce into letting her join Club X.

"Lots of those students are in the debating society, too," Bill explained. He gave Elizabeth an apologetic grimace for stretching the truth to the breaking point. "They're probably just practicing for an upcoming tournament."

"Right," Todd said encouragingly. "The big tournament is coming up soon, so they're all practicing really hard."

"That girl there," Mrs. Vlasaya asked, pointing at Jessica. "She is your twin sister, yes? Is she the head of this debating society?"

"Well, I guess you could say that," Elizabeth

replied. She took a deep breath and let it out slowly. She felt ridiculous, but at least she, Todd, and Bill had managed to provide some kind of explanation for the chaotic scene.

"OK, OK!" Bruce's voice suddenly quelled the noisy arguments all around him. He looked at Jessica. "If you really want to try getting in, you've got it."

Immediately, all the girls sent up a loud cheer.

"Way to go, Jessica!" Denise Hadley exclaimed.

Jessica looked around with a beaming smile, and lifted her fist in a power salute. The girls all cheered again, and then the crowd began to drift away.

"I guess it's over," Todd said. "Let's get on line for lunch."

Elizabeth snapped back to attention and nodded at her guests. "Right this way," she said, gesturing with one hand.

"In Japan, our students debate sitting down," Mrs. Ochiba said primly.

"Passionate argument is all very well," Mr. Turner-Cox observed. "But it helps to have a moderator. Keeps things more civilized."

"We do not debate so loudly in India," Mr. Srinivasen said. "At least, not during a meal."

Chagrined, Elizabeth cast around in her mind for a graceful way to change the subject. The sooner they stopped discussing American debating technique, the better.

"Speaking of meals," Bill said in his friendly, easygoing way, "there's a really excellent one today. Chili burgers. They're the best."

35

Elizabeth glanced back at the crowded tables. Jessica was still talking to Bruce, and she wore a triumphant smile.

Elizabeth grudgingly admitted to herself that Jessica had proven an important point by breaking down Bruce's obnoxious gender restriction.

But as she turned away, the expression on Bruce's face stopped her. He had a nasty gleam in his eyes and it made Elizabeth nervous.

Jessica might have won the first round, but to what extent would Bruce go to win the next one?

Four

"Tonight's the night," Jessica crowed as she slammed her locker door shut at the end of the day. She leaned against it and gave Lila and Amy a satisfied smile.

Students leaving for the buses streamed past them. Amy shouldered her book bag and looked at the ceiling. "So, when are you going to Bruce's?" she asked.

"*We*'re supposed to be there at eight," Jessica said.

"Actually . . ." Amy glanced quickly at Lila, and then at Jessica. Lila let her breath out slowly.

Jessica frowned at her friends. "You two *are* coming, right? That's what we agreed."

"Oh, Jessica." Lila sighed. "I never *really* wanted to be in Bruce's stupid club. I just wanted him to back down. And he did."

"Talk about backing down!" Jessica said. She

37

shook her head in disbelief. "What is with you two? You *have* to go through with this."

Amy rolled her eyes. "I changed my mind, OK? But *you* should definitely go to the meeting, Jess. Everyone's counting on you.

"Great!" Jessica strode down the hall, with her friends right behind her. "You two back out, but you know perfectly well *I* can't. Everyone heard Bruce tell me I could try to get in, and if I don't show up, they'll all say he was right. That Susan Butcher, Sandra Day O'Connor, and Sally Ride are just flukes, and that most girls are gutless chickens."

"You're packed full of guts," Lila said with a grin. "Go on. You're the one who really wanted to get in from the beginning."

They all stepped outside into the afternoon sunshine. "Maybe Bruce was right about you two," Jessica said indignantly. "Well, fine. I *am* going through with it. By myself."

"Good," Amy said.

"Good," Lila echoed with another smile.

"Good good good," Jessica said, storming off in disgust. "But don't expect me to tell you all about it!" she threw back over her shoulder. "Because I won't!"

Jessica was furious—and filled with a sense of purpose. Almost every girl at Sweet Valley High was counting on her. And without doubt, almost every boy was watching to see if she would go through with it.

Clenching her jaw, Jessica walked to the parking lot and climbed into the Jeep. She realized that deep down inside, she probably had always known that Lila and Amy wouldn't want to join Bruce's club. Even though they liked to put on a rebellious act, they really were content to play it safe. Both Lila and Amy probably assumed that Bruce would force them to do something really embarrassing or stupid or dangerous. The thought that one of them might have to pull the fire alarm, or something comparable, had them both running scared.

"But I'm not afraid of *anything* Bruce can dish up," she muttered, gunning the engine.

Two senior girls walking nearby turned at the sound of the racing engine and stared at Jessica in alarm. Jessica realized she must have had a very fierce expression on her face.

"I'm not going to run you down," Jessica called out to them. *But if Bruce gets in my way,* she added to herself, *I won't promise the same thing.*

Elizabeth took a long swallow of her root beer. After the diplomacy she had been practicing all afternoon with the visiting teachers, she was exhausted. Dropping in at the Dairi Burger with her friends was the best way to decompress. Todd sat next to her, Enid was on the other side of the booth with her boyfriend, Hugh Grayson, and Winston Egbert and Maria Santelli had squeezed in on the ends.

"Let me ask you guys something," Elizabeth

said, looking around with a smile. "Do *you* think women and men are equal in all things?"

Winston shook his head emphatically. "No way. Women have nicer hair."

"Come on, Win," Maria said. "Be serious."

"I am serious," he insisted. "You girls have great hair. Mine's weird."

Elizabeth laughed. "But honestly, I couldn't get over how many guys were agreeing with Bruce today in that huge argument in the cafeteria."

"Look, we all know what Bruce is like," Todd said grimly.

Elizabeth nodded. "We sure do!" She knew just what was going through Todd's mind. Just a short time ago, Phi Epsilon, the fraternity that many of their friends belonged to, had begun offering bids to new pledges. Bruce and Todd had each put up two friends for membership. What started as a small rivalry to make the most difficult hazing tasks for the pledges had escalated into a one-on-one battle between Bruce and Todd that almost broke up the fraternity completely. Afterwards, Todd had admitted to being embarrassed that he had let Bruce goad him into the feud. It was an unfortunate fact that Bruce's strong personality allowed him to take charge of almost any situation.

"And a lot of guys think he's cool, so they want to be on his side," Winston added. "Even if they don't really believe in what he's saying."

"Well, I think that's stupid," Enid declared, her eyes flashing. "If you can't make up your own mind and form your own opinions, you might as well be a robot."

Hugh looked blankly at her. "Is that what you think? Then I agree with you, Enid," he said in a monotone.

Everyone laughed, but Elizabeth still felt the need to get at the heart of the matter. "This club issue raises a lot of questions. For example, I know I like it when Todd opens the door for me—"

"That's just politeness," Winston said.

"But isn't it also a subtle way of saying that women can't open doors?" Maria challenged.

The boys were silent for a moment. "If you don't want us to open doors for you," Hugh began, and then stopped. None of them knew how to resolve such a complicated question then and there, but Elizabeth knew that her friends were thoughtful and serious enough to keep thinking it through on their own.

"You know," Enid said worriedly, "it's possible we're wrong about Bruce."

"You're not sticking up for him, are you?" Todd asked in surprise.

Enid shook her head. "No, I still think he's a rat. What I mean is, what if *he* really doesn't believe the things he's saying? How could he, honestly? Look, women have already *proven* themselves equal to men. He can't seriously ignore the facts. So what if he's *pretending* to be sexist, and deliberately starting an argument?"

"That *would* be just like him," Elizabeth mused. "He loves to manipulate people."

"Well, whether he believes what he says or not,

almost the whole school is talking about it now," Todd said.

Elizabeth gave her friends an odd smile. "I wish I could say that Jessica is a really strong feminist. But I think the truth is that she just hates having anyone tell her she can't do something."

"And Bruce told her she couldn't be in his club," Enid concluded. "He probably just made up that rule as a way of provoking people. It sure worked with Jessica."

"But now he's agreed to let her try for membership," Winston reminded them all.

Elizabeth nodded thoughtfully. Bruce never gave up without a fight. And Jessica never let anything stop her from doing what she wanted to do.

It sounded to Elizabeth like a recipe for disaster.

At five minutes before eight o'clock, Jessica was driving up the tree-lined road that wound up the hill overlooking Sweet Valley. On either side, large, expensive homes and their landscaped yards were tucked behind stone walls and fences. When she pulled the Jeep into the driveway of the Patmans' lavish estate, Jessica took a deep breath and let it out slowly. She was ready.

Bruce's black Porsche was parked in front of the wide steps. Behind it were Ronnie's old green Camaro and Tad's battered VW Rabbit.

"The gang's all here," Jessica said to herself as she climbed down from the Jeep's high seat.

The front door opened, and Bruce was framed

42

by the light pouring out from behind him. "So, you did come," he said.

"When will you ever learn, Bruce," Jessica replied breezily. "I always do what I say I will."

Bruce laughed. "Just remember you said that, OK?"

"Why?" Jessica asked as she followed him inside.

Leading the way downstairs to the basement den, Bruce shook his head and laughed. "You'll see."

Jessica followed Bruce into the spacious room that he used as his private living room. Two comfortable leather couches occupied the center of the room, and a high-tech entertainment system took up one whole wall. Tad and Ronnie were lounging on the couches, eating taco chips from a bag. They looked up at Jessica and grinned.

"The new recruit," Bruce announced dramatically.

Jessica felt a ripple of nervous excitement. She wasn't completely sure what she had gotten herself into, but she was sure it would be a challenge. Keeping her chin up and her smile confident, Jessica sat down in a canvas deck chair and folded her arms. She was slightly apprehensive, but she was beginning to enjoy herself. *This must be what Sam feels right before a race on a dangerous course*, she thought excitedly.

"So, here I am," she said, her voice steady. "Now let me in on the big secret."

The three boys were silent for a few moments, assessing her. Jessica felt her face grow warm under their scrutiny. Every second that went by made her more and more determined to pass whatever test they had in store for her.

"First of all," Bruce began, "everything that you hear and see stays here in this room. You have to swear not to talk to anyone about what we do."

"OK," Jessica said easily.

"Anyone," Tad repeated. "That means your sister, too."

Jessica grimaced. "I don't have to tell Liz everything that happens to me, you know."

Bruce sent the other two boys a crooked grin, but he shrugged. "Second, once you're in, you're in for life."

His serious tone almost made Jessica laugh, but all three of the boys were looking at her without a trace of humor. Whatever she was getting into, she realized she was getting into it up to her neck. The sensible part of her wanted to put the brakes on right then before she made any more promises, and find out exactly what she was committing to. But the stronger, adventurous part of her nature told her to go for it.

"I understand," she said in a cool, detached voice.

"Great." Bruce stood up, and nodded toward the far end of the room. "Let's get started."

Jessica followed Bruce, and Tad and Ronnie followed her.

Bruce led the way to a table in the corner, and switched on a jointed architect's lamp so that its beam shone down on the center. In the circle of bright light was a roulette wheel, with four equal

44

sectors marked off with a piece of cardboard. On each piece was a name: Bruce, Ronnie, Tad—and Jessica. An arrow was painted on the rim of the wheel.

"What is this?" she asked, noticing that her throat was dry. "The wheel of fortune?"

"Something like that," Ronnie snickered.

Bruce reached out and gave the wheel an experimental spin, and then stopped it with one finger. "This is how we get our kicks at Club X. If the wheel stops with the arrow pointing at your name, you perform a dare."

"What kind of dare?" Jessica asked. Her gaze flicked back and forth across the boys' faces. She had already begun to suspect that this was the nature of Club X.

"Anything that involves a risk," Bruce explained, watching her steadily.

Jessica shrugged. Risk could mean anything from hang gliding to cheating on a test. Between Phi Epsilon and Pi Beta Alpha pledge weeks, there were plenty of pranks at Sweet Valley High. But Jessica suspected there must be something more to Club X's dares than simple locker-room raids. And the boys were obviously enjoying keeping her in suspense as long as possible.

"Risk. Could that mean something like setting off the fire alarms at school?" she asked.

Tad grinned. "Yeah, could be."

"That was just a little one," Ronnie said. "Just to make the day a little more interesting."

"So I *was* right yesterday," Jessica said to Bruce.

"You certainly were," he answered lightly.

"OK," Jessica went on, still maintaining her un-ruffled poise. "So you have to perform a dare. What happens if you don't do it? You get kicked out?"

Bruce smiled. "I told you, Jessica. Once you're in, you're in for life."

Jessica was beginning to lose her patience. Her nerves were stretched thin with anticipation, rest-lessness, and anxiety.

"Quit the mystery routine, guys," Jessica mut-tered. "What happens?"

"If you can't perform the dare—for any rea-son," Ronnie explained, "we add another space to the wheel."

"With your name on it," Tad said.

"So the odds are greater that you'll have to per-form the next dare, too," Jessica concluded. "I see."

"How do you like it now?" Bruce asked taunting her. "You wanted to play with the boys, Jessica. Now you're in with us and you can't get out."

Jessica met Bruce's challenging look with a com-posed smile. "Sounds like fun," she said evenly. "Why should I want to get out?"

Ronnie and Tad laughed in admiration, but Bruce's smile faded. "OK," he said sharply. "Let's get to it."

"Let Jessica spin," Tad suggested.

"Fine." Bruce held up both hands and backed away from the wheel. "We just take turns making up the dares. Whoever thinks of a good dare gets to assign it. But whoever wants to spin the wheel can. Tonight, ladies first."

Jessica shot him a hard glance and then reached for the handle of the wheel. She backed it up before giving it a hard twist. The ratchets clicked rapidly, and the names spun by in a blur. Gradually, the wheel slowed, coming to a stop with Jessica's name under the arrow. Her heart jumped once in her chest, and settled into a strong, quick pulse as the adrenaline coursed through her veins. Jessica looked up to see the three boys looking at her expectantly.

"OK. What's my dare?" she asked.

"I came up with a good one, and we agreed on it before you got here," Bruce said, turning a chair around and straddling it. "What you have to do is relatively simple. Just drive down to the bottom of the hill. It's about a mile."

Jessica narrowed her eyes. "What's the catch?"

"Without headlights," Ronnie said, his eyes glowing. "It should be pretty dark by now."

"No problem," Jessica said. She was determined not to let her nervousness show. It was frightening, but it was a rush, too. Straightening her back, she turned and headed back up the stairs and out the front door.

"Do you go with me, or what?" she asked as she opened the door of the Jeep.

"I'll be at the bottom of the hill," Bruce said. "Tad and Ronnie will drive down and stop at two other spots on the way. Just to make sure you don't . . ."

"Cheat?" Jessica said. "Don't worry about me. I can handle it fine."

"OK," Bruce said with a nod. "See you down there."

As the three boys got in their cars and drove off, Jessica climbed into the driver's seat. Her hand trembled slightly, but she gripped the steering wheel hard and breathed deeply.

She knew that driving down the hill without headlights was risky, but not really dangerous. This was certainly not as crazy as some of the other things she had done in her life. But on the other hand, the Jeep was new, and if she even scratched it, she knew she would have some explaining to do. Sure, it was a stupid thing to do, she reasoned. But she couldn't back down at this point. Bruce and the others would never let her live it down. They would see it as proving their ridiculous point that girls, and Jessica in particular, didn't have the same courage and daring that boys did. It would only seem to prove that Bruce was right about her not having the guts for Club X. The other day Bruce had said that in a dangerous situation a girl would just cry for help. Jessica wouldn't cry for help. She wouldn't give Bruce that satisfaction.

For a few minutes she sat and let her eyes grow accustomed to the darkness. When she decided that the boys were in position, she started the engine.

"No problem," she whispered.

The adrenaline was still rippling through her like tiny jolts of electricity. She was psyched for the challenge.

Carefully, she put the Jeep into gear and

pressed lightly on the accelerator. The engine responded instantly, and she drove out of the Patmans' broad circular driveway and turned onto the street.

The only light came from homes scattered back behind the trees. But the pale surface of road gleamed faintly in the moonlight. Slowly, Jessica began the one-mile drive down the hill, and breathed a silent prayer of gratitude that she knew the route so well.

At the first turn, Jessica kept close to the edge of the road. Fortunately, there were no oncoming headlights, but Jessica was afraid that an animal might dart out in front of her wheels. A driveway loomed darkly among the trees to her right, and then was past.

"No problem," Jessica whispered again, talking quietly to herself to keep her confidence up.

When she passed another driveway, a pair of headlights flashed on briefly and went dark. She could just make out the silhouette of Ronnie's Camaro. "Checkpoint one," Jessica said.

Her hands were steady on the wheel as she passed the second checkpoint and Tad flashed his lights. There was only a short stretch of road left, with one more turn near the bottom.

Suddenly, a dark shape scurried out from the bushes on the left. Jessica stepped on the brakes as a cat crossed the road and disappeared into the underbrush again. For a moment, she imagined what Sam would say if he knew what she was doing. He faced danger all the time, but he went into every race fully prepared, with a helmet, protective clothing, his bike in top condition, in short, with every possible guard against the unexpected. Jessica felt momentarily ashamed. Sam would never do what she was doing.

But then again, she reasoned, he didn't have as much at stake as she did. Sam had gotten into bike racing for kicks, not to prove anything to anyone. Jessica licked her lips and went forward again.

Finally, she rounded the last bend and pulled off onto the gravel shoulder. The headlights of Bruce's car turned on, and shone in through her windshield. Jessica allowed herself a smile of victory as she turned the engine of the Jeep off.

Bruce passed in front of his headlights, his footsteps crunching on the gravel, and stopped at Jessica's door.

"You did it, Wakefield," he said. His expression was impossible to read in the glare of the Porsche's lights.

Jessica opened her door and got out. Her legs were trembling slightly, but she managed to stand up straight. She had done it. It had been easy, really.

"Surprised?" she asked as Ronnie and Tad both pulled in behind her.

"You never surprise me, Jessica," Bruce said with a soft laugh.

"Way to go, Jessica," Ronnie said.

Bruce walked back to his car and came back, holding something in his hands. He held it out to her.

"Welcome to Club X," he said, handing her a black leather jacket.

A surge of triumph lifted Jessica's spirits even higher. She let out a laugh. "Thanks. I hope it's the right size."

"Put it on," Tad suggested.

She shrugged into it, relishing the creak of the leather as she bent her arms in the sleeves. "How do I look?"

"Like a member of the club," Bruce said. "Oh, there's just one more thing. We use the roulette for the high-risk dares, but being in the club means getting out there and taking risks *all* the time. If you see a chance, you have to go for it. We'll all be watching. See you tomorrow night."

"That's it? We're done?" Jessica asked, momentarily let down.

"That's it," Bruce agreed. "You've done it. Remember the rules."

"See you tomorrow," Ronnie said in a friendly voice.

Jessica nodded. "Yeah. Right. See you guys in school."

Slowly she climbed back behind the wheel of the Jeep. For a moment she was tempted to drive off without her lights, just to prove she was even tougher than they thought. But then she remembered how close she had come to hitting the cat, and she switched the headlights on, tooted the horn, and drove off.

As she drove, Jessica thought less and less of the risk and more and more of the thrill of having proved herself. "Cry for help!" Jessica said with a breathless laugh. "Eat your heart out, Bruce."

Danger. It was like an animal, Jessica mused. It could lash out and hurt you, or it could be controlled. It was all in your attitude. And she knew she was the sort of person who had the right attitude. She felt powerful and strong and ready for anything. Jessica was smiling as she pulled into the driveway, and once inside she bounded up the stairs two at a time.

"Can I come in?" she asked, opening Elizabeth's bedroom door.

"You're in." Elizabeth looked up from her book. Her eyes widened as she took in Jessica's expression. "You look pretty excited."

"I am," Jessica admitted, sitting on her sister's bed and pulling a pillow into her lap. She was bursting with the news about Club X. Now that she had stormed the barricades, she had to share her victory with someone.

"Listen," she said. "Promise not to tell anyone, OK?"

"OK, what is it?" Elizabeth said.

Quickly, Jessica filled her sister in on what had happened. Elizabeth's expression became more skeptical by the moment, until Jessica revealed what her dare had been.

"You didn't do it, did you?" Elizabeth gasped.

"Yes," Jessica said, waving aside Elizabeth's disapproval. "But I figured it all out. I'm sure that tonight was a test. You know, like an initiation, or a hazing. I'm sure that from now on the dares

52

will be really simple stuff. You know Bruce is mostly talk."

Elizabeth was shaking her head. "Jess, that was really dumb. You could have hurt someone, or hurt yourself. It was dangerous."

"Don't worry, Liz," Jessica said with a confident smile. "Like I said, it'll be smooth sailing from now on. And remember, not a word, not a *syllable* to anyone."

Elizabeth lowered her eyes. "OK," she said quietly. "But I wish you'd quit now. You've proved your point, so why stay?"

"Because," Jessica said, feeling a flash of annoyance at her sister. Elizabeth wasn't at all proud of how Jessica had mastered the situation. Elizabeth couldn't see what an important step Jessica had taken in proving that women were as brave and daring as men. Jessica could see there were more battles ahead, but Elizabeth couldn't. That was typical. "I just want to."

Elizabeth sighed. "OK. You never listen to me, anyway. Oh—before I forget, Sam called. Are you going to tell him about this club?"

Jessica's heart leaped at the mention of Sam's name. Without answering her sister, she jumped off the bed and ran through the bathroom that connected their rooms. She dialed the number of Sam's dormitory, anxious to hear his voice.

But as she listened to the faraway ringing on the line, she decided she wouldn't tell him anything about Club X. Not just yet, anyway.

Five

Jessica woke up on Friday with a feeling of anticipation. As she opened her eyes, her gaze fell on the new black leather jacket that was slung over a chair. A contented smile spread across her face.

"Mmmm," she murmured, rubbing her face on her pillow. She could almost taste the attention she was going to draw when she walked into school that morning wearing her Club X jacket.

Briefly, her thoughts flickered back to her phone conversation with Sam the night before. When he had asked her what she had been up to lately, she had filled him in on all the recent gossip from school, on a tennis match she had played with Steven and won, and on her plans to see a movie with Lila. But she had steered clear of mentioning Club X and her rivalry with

Bruce. Sam knew that Jessica had once dated Bruce, and after what they had gone through over Jessica's crush on Brandon Hunter, she didn't want to give Sam any reason to feel jealous.

But Jessica didn't want to admit to herself the *real* reason for her not having told Sam about Club X. And that was that she had a fairly strong suspicion that Sam would think it was a bad idea. Sam would never understand the point in maximizing risk, which was exactly what Jessica knew she was doing.

You have to create the danger, then control it, and your fear of it, Jessica said to herself. But she couldn't imagine saying that to Sam.

Wrinkling her nose in annoyance, Jessica dragged herself out of bed and into the shower. As the water streamed down her face, she resolved to put Sam out of her mind. He wasn't in town and there was no point in wishing he were, or in worrying what he would say if he came home and found out about Club X. By the time she was ready for school, she was in a buoyant mood again.

"Everyone is going to go nuts when they see this jacket," she told Elizabeth gleefully as they drove into the Sweet Valley High parking lot.

"I think you're the one who's nuts," Elizabeth replied.

Jessica rolled her eyes. "Oh, come on, Liz. Don't be mad. It's just for kicks," she said, snapping and unsnapping a pocket flap on her jacket. She twisted her head around to catch a glimpse of the X on her back. Then she grinned. She had won.

Waving a carefree goodbye to her sister, Jessica ran ahead and bounded up the stairs to the main entrance. Inside, Maria Santelli and DeeDee Gordon were putting up a poster for an upcoming school play.

"Hi," Jessica said, walking past them with a casual smile.

Maria turned to say hello, but then let out a tiny scream. "Jessica! You're in the club!"

"Oh," Jessica stopped and glanced down at her jacket as though she had forgotten about it. She shrugged. "Yes, I said I could get in, and I did."

Just then Amy and Lila walked by and stopped dead when they saw Jessica's jacket.

"I can't believe it!" Amy gasped.

Lila took Jessica's arm and turned her around to examine the bold white X. "You did it," she said, smiling wryly. "Congratulations."

"So tell all," Amy said in a breathless voice. "What did you have to do?"

"Yeah," Lila said as several other girls joined the group. "Spill it."

Even if Jessica had been alone with Lila and Amy, she wouldn't have told them a thing. It wasn't only her vow of secrecy that kept her silent. She was still irked that her friends had pushed her to join Bruce's club, but then had chickened out themselves at the last moment. She was going to keep them in suspense for as long as she could. It would be her revenge.

"Sorry," she said, beginning to walk away. "If you join, you'll find out everything."

"Come on, Jess," Amy said, running after her eagerly. "We won't tell anyone."

Jessica laughed. "Right, Amy. Nobody can keep a secret like you can."

Amy stopped and pouted, but Jessica continued walking down the hall. From each side, surprised students took in the fact that she was wearing a Club X jacket. Some of them smiled, and some looked indifferent. But Jessica knew perfectly well that everyone *noticed*.

"Hey, Jess," came a familiar voice.

She glanced back. Michael Harris, a senior, was jogging to catch up to her. Jessica gave him a friendly smile. He was a dirt-bike racer, too, and a friend of Sam's. In fact, she had met Sam through Michael and his girlfriend, April Dawson.

"I'm totally impressed," he said, eyeing her appreciatively. "If there's one girl in this school who can do *anything*, it's you."

"Thanks." Jessica arched her eyebrows and grinned. Being the center of attention was one of her favorite pastimes.

Michael shoved his hands in his pockets. "Do you think I could get into Club X? You have to do some kind of dare, right?"

"Maybe," she drawled, pleased to see that the rumor was still hard at work. "I can't tell you too much, but you might be able to get in, if you have what it takes. Talk to Bruce if you're interested."

With that, she waved and headed for her

locker, a smile of pure satisfaction on her lips. Joining Club X was beginning to look like the best thing she had done in ages. First of all, it had given her a chance to show up Bruce. Secondly, it was making her more popular than ever. And thirdly, it might actually be *fun* going through some of the dares.

By lunchtime, Jessica and her membership in Club X were the talk of school. The moment she arrived in the cafeteria and sat at her usual table, she was surrounded by friends.

"Was it hard?" Jean asked, her eyes wide.

Jessica snapped open a can of diet soda. "I can't tell you anything about it."

"Come on, a hint," Amy begged.

"Nope. Sorry." Jessica took a long sip.

"I heard Michael Harris might want to join," Lila announced.

"He's such a hunk," Amy said with a shiver.

"Cool it, Amy. He's taken," Maria laughed. "And don't forget about Barry. Remember him?"

Amy smiled a slow, catlike smile. "Of course I do. But I can still admire from a distance, can't I?"

Jessica wondered if Michael really would join, and for that matter, who else might. If the only members were Bruce, Tad, Ronnie, and herself, it might become pretty boring. As she thought over the more adventurous students she knew, her thoughts returned to Sam for the second time that day. Sam certainly was adventurous. Dirt-bike racing wasn't exactly for the faint-hearted, even though he always took safety very seriously. *Perhaps he* would *join if he knew about Club X*, she thought. She could picture him perfectly in a black leather jacket, and thought he would look like a young James Dean.

I will tell him about it, she decided. But as Bruce sauntered into the cafeteria and bestowed a glittering smile on the tableful of girls, her heart skipped a beat. She hated to admit it, but Bruce was totally gorgeous, even if he was her arch-rival. Matching wits with him, waiting to see who would blink first, was a thrill in itself. Sam might not appreciate that aspect of Club X very much.

I will tell Sam, she vowed. *But not yet.*

Elizabeth sat at the large metal table in the school newspaper office that afternoon, gazing into space. In the typewriter in front of her was a blank sheet of paper. Her piece on Sweet Valley High's foreign guests was due tomorrow but she just couldn't concentrate. She had a few scribbled notes on a pad beside her, but they didn't amount to anything. She had picked up plenty of interesting facts from the time she had spent with the members of the teachers' delegation, but her observations wouldn't come together into a coherent form. There was one note at the bottom of the pad that didn't pertain to her article, and now she turned her attention to that. Maybe she should try to work on something else, she thought.

The note was two simple words: Project Youth. Project Youth was a service run by a local community group; it was partly staffed by teenagers who answered phone calls from other, troubled teens. The idea behind the hot line was that teens with problems would find it easier to talk to their peers than to adult counselors. Elizabeth had written about the hot line before; in fact, she had interviewed both Amy and Barry, who volunteered there after school whenever they could. Now she was considering writing an update on the various programs that were sponsored by the community center.

With a frown, Elizabeth picked up her pencil. The first thing to do would be find out if there were any new hot-line helpers, and talk to them. Elizabeth took a breath and tried to think of her angle. But it was no use. She just couldn't get up any enthusiasm today.

The truth was that her mind was stalled on Jessica and Club X. Even if she hadn't promised Jessica she would keep Club X's rules and actions a secret, Elizabeth wouldn't have discussed it with anyone. To her mind, the club was just one big foolhardy stunt. The less public and private encouragement Bruce got, the better.

Elizabeth sighed and shifted in her seat. If Bruce was serious about women being less than men, and he really *did* hate the thought of Jessica having made it into Club X, chances were good that he wasn't going to give in gracefully. Elizabeth had seen Bruce play tennis often enough to know that he never gave up without a wicked fight. If the score was against him, he would come back at his opponent with furious concentration, and if possible, pound his rival into the ground. His having allowed Jessica into Club X made Elizabeth suspicious. Jessica may have been too blinded by her triumph to realize it, but Elizabeth was concerned that Bruce was up to something.

I should try to get her to quit, Elizabeth told herself firmly.

Elizabeth focused her attention once more on her newspaper column. She was pecking half-heartedly at the typewriter keys when the office door opened and Todd stuck his head in.

"Hey, almost finished?" he asked.

"Hi. Not exactly." Elizabeth pulled her blond hair into a ponytail and lifted it off her neck. It was hot in the office, and she was restless.

Todd came in and perched on the edge of the table. "It's almost four o'clock. I thought we could stop by the Dairi Burger for a soda or something."

"Well . . ." Elizabeth stared at the paper in her typewriter, and let out a frustrated sigh. "OK, I give up."

She yanked the paper out, balled it up, and tossed it in the wastebasket.

"She shoots, she scores!" Todd said, raising two fingers in the air. He smiled expectantly at her. Then he looked concerned. "Is something wrong? Or am I just really boring?"

Elizabeth smiled tiredly. "Oh, I'm sorry. I guess I was spacing out there for a second."

"What's wrong?" he asked, walking over and smoothing the bangs off her forehead.

"Nothing." Elizabeth looked up at him and smiled. "You wouldn't by any chance be interested in joining Club X, would you?"

"Me?" Todd laughed. "Come on, give me a break. After that last Phi Epsilon rush, you know how I feel about Bruce. Club X will have to do without me. Especially if the whole thing is about taking dares."

Elizabeth darted a swift glance at him. "Where did you hear that?"

"It's the rumor going around," Todd said. "And I know what kind of dares Bruce likes. You can't exactly call them lighthearted. So don't worry, I'm not about to ask if I can become a member of Club X."

Elizabeth let another smile flash across her face. "I know. Just . . . don't change your mind, OK?"

"Come on," Todd said, putting his arms around her. "Let's go get a soda."

"OK," Elizabeth answered. She hugged him tight. "Let's go."

No matter how much Todd tried to cheer her up, though, Elizabeth still felt troubled about Jessica and Bruce. And when Jessica ran out of the house after dinner, saying she was going over to Lila's house to study, Elizabeth felt a sinking sensation in the pit of her stomach. She was sure Jessica was going to another meeting of Club X.

I could call Bruce's house and leave a message that she has to come home right away, Elizabeth told herself as she scooped some ice cream into a dish in the kitchen.

She paused, licked the spoon, and stared into space. She could say it was an emergency. Once Jessica got home and found there wasn't an emergency, she would be angry, but at least she would have missed the Club X meeting.

Elizabeth put down her spoon and picked up the phone. But when she heard the dial tone, she hesitated. Jessica might have been correct in thinking the dares to come wouldn't be as dangerous as her first one had been. And Jessica *could* certainly handle herself. Elizabeth was pretty certain that free-spirited as she was, Jessica was also sensible enough not to do anything illegal or downright crazy.

Elizabeth put the phone down and resumed eating her ice cream. It just wasn't right to try to run her sister's life. But still, she would like to talk about her dilemma with someone. She thought of calling Enid but quickly realized that her promise of secrecy ruled that out. An impartial stranger would really be the best.

Elizabeth dropped her spoon into the empty bowl with a clatter. "Hot line," she said out loud.

Elizabeth reached for the phone book and scanned the blue social services pages at the front. As soon as she found the number, she dialed.

"Project Youth," a young male voice said.

"Hi," Elizabeth said. "I need some advice."

"Sure, what's the problem?"

"Do I have to tell you my name, or what school

I go to, or anything like that?" Elizabeth asked nervously.

"Only if you want to," the boy said in a friendly tone. "What's on your mind?"

Elizabeth coiled the phone cord around one finger. "I think my sister's getting involved in something stupid," she explained. "I don't want her to think I'm butting into her life, but I want her to stop doing what she's doing. Does that make sense?"

"I know what you mean. Does it involve drugs or alcohol? Because if it does, you *should* butt in, whether you want to or not."

Elizabeth shook her head. "No. It's just . . ."

"Is she smart? I mean, can she take care of herself?"

A dozen memories flashed through Elizabeth's mind. More than once Jessica had needed to be bailed out of a disaster. But she had a kind of street-smartness that had gotten her through an awful lot of scrapes.

"Yes, she can take care of herself," Elizabeth admitted.

"Well, this is how I feel," her anonymous friend went on. "If she's really hurting herself, or hurting anyone else, you should step in. Otherwise, I would let her alone. If she's smart, she'll probably figure out on her own that she should quit what she's doing. Then you'll both win, without you two getting into a big hassle about it, right?"

"You're right," Elizabeth said warmly. "If I know my sister, something else will capture her attention any day now and she'll drop this current infatuation! Thanks for listening."

"That's what we're here for," he replied. "Call anytime."

Six

Jessica followed Bruce down the stairs to his den. From the cars parked in the driveway, she knew that Tad and Ronnie were already there. She didn't know exactly what to expect from her second night as a member of Club X, but she knew she would be ready for it.

"Let's do it," Bruce said, switching on the light over the roulette wheel.

In the circle of the light from the lamp, the wheel looked almost expectant, as though it knew the power it had over the four people gathered around it.

"Anyone think of a good dare, yet?" Tad asked. "I tried to come up with one," he added sheepishly, "but I couldn't think of anything."

Bruce laughed. "Don't worry, big guy. I've got a good one."

"Can I spin the wheel?" Jessica asked, already

feeling a slight thrill of anticipation running through her.

Bruce nodded, a sly grin on his face. "Sure, Jessica. Go right ahead."

Jessica heard the smugness in his voice. He sounded as if he were in possession of some great secret. Jessica shrugged. *He's probably just psyched like I am*, she thought. Jessica gave the wheel a sharp twist.

The fast, furious buzzing of clicks sounded ominous in the silence, as the cardboard sectors that comprised the wheel spun by in a blur. The wheel gradually slowed, and their four names became almost legible.

Ronnie, Bruce, Tad, Jessica, Ronnie. The wheel turned more and more slowly, each name passing the arrow and just sliding by.

Jessica held her breath as her name approached the arrow. Bruce was watching with a gleam of delight in his dark-lashed eyes.

Click, click, click. Jessica's name slowed by the arrow, and then ticked by. Then the section with Ronnie's name on it clicked under the arrow, and the wheel stopped.

An expression of surprise and disappointment crossed Bruce's face, and then was quickly masked, but not before Jessica noticed it.

"What's wrong?" she asked him, smiling archly. "You look bummed out."

"No, I'm not," Bruce said. "Why should I be?"

Jessica smiled to herself. Bruce was so transparent. Without a doubt, he had been hoping she would have to perform the night's dare, and without a doubt, he had been hoping that she would fail it.

"So," Ronnie said, taking a breath. "What do I have to do?"

"You're going to go swimming," Bruce announced abruptly.

"Good thing it's hot tonight," Tad said with a throaty chuckle.

"Swimming where?" Jessica asked. She had gone to the beach after school, and was still wearing her bikini under her clothes. Who knew? She might even join Ronnie and go swimming herself.

"We're going to the pool at the community park," Bruce said, heading for the stairs.

"But it's closed at night," Jessica said.

Bruce stopped and looked over his shoulder. "So?"

Ronnie laughed. "So I guess I'll have to climb the fence, right?"

"And dive off the high dive," Bruce added, taking the stairs two at a time.

"All right!" Tad said.

Jessica's pulse began to quicken, and a flush of excitement brightened her cheeks. She knew the pool wasn't lit at night, and that Ronnie would be diving out into darkness. She could just imagine the thoughts that would be racing through his mind as he psyched himself up for a blind leap. And then Jessica experienced a ripple of nervousness. There was also a little matter of trespassing involved. *Fraternity and sorority pranks were never this outrageous*, she thought.

Outside, they each got into their cars, and

headed down into Sweet Valley. The community park was in a secluded, wooded area, and the pool itself was in the middle, surrounded by trees and a high fence.

The four of them parked their cars in a shadowy corner at the edge of the park. A light breeze rustled the leaves and branches overhead as they silently walked the gravel path toward the pool.

Ronnie was in front, walking quickly. Thinking of her dark drive the night before, Jessica could guess what he was feeling: a mixture of nervousness and exhilaration, and a determination to complete the dare successfully. Jessica almost envied him!

Ahead of them, the chain link fence loomed up against a slightly luminous sky. The faint lapping of water reached their ears. They stood by the fence opposite the deep end, where the tall platform of the high dive towered above their heads.

"Go for it," Bruce said in a low voice.

Jessica could feel the adrenaline zinging through her as Ronnie scaled the fence. He swung himself over the top, and then dropped lightly to the ground. Once there, he stripped off his T-shirt and jeans.

Jessica twined her fingers through the wire, and leaned forward as Ronnie began to climb the ladder. As her eyes adjusted to the dark she could see better, but still, Ronnie was nothing more than a shadowy form as he went higher and higher against the black silhouette of the diving platform. The breeze kicked up again, making the water in the pool slap and gurgle against the drains. Jessica licked her lips, her eyes riveted on Ronnie.

At the top, Ronnie walked to the end of the platform and paused. He was only a tall black shape against the twinkling stars.

"Go on, Edwards," Bruce said under his breath.

"You can do it," Jessica whispered. For a moment she closed her eyes and imagined herself up there with Ronnie, staring down into the deep, black pool. She could feel both the danger of the darkness and of the illegality of the dare.

Ronnie raised his arms, and then leaped out into space. A second later, they all heard the splash as he plunged into the water. Jessica caught her breath. The night was completely silent except for the slapping, swishing backwash from Ronnie's dive.

Then there was another splash as Ronnie shot up out of the water and heaved himself onto the edge of the pool.

"Yes!" he shouted, throwing his head back to shake his wet hair from his face.

Jessica let out her breath. "Wow. That was great."

"I bet you're glad that wasn't you, Wakefield," Bruce said.

Jessica turned to face him in the darkness. "Oh, really? You think I couldn't have done that?"

"No," he said, a smile in his voice.

"Watch me," Jessica replied.

Without another word, Jessica began to climb the fence. The wire bent and swayed as she hauled herself up and over. When both legs were over, she climbed down a few feet and then jumped to the ground.

Ronnie was still shaking the water from his hair and wiping it off his arms. "What are you doing?" he asked as Jessica dropped down beside him.

"It's a nice night for a swim," she replied. She eased off her jacket, kicked off her shoes, pulled her shirt off over her head, and stepped out of her jeans. Then she shot a glance back at Bruce and Tad standing on the other side of the fence.

"Last one in's a rotten egg," she taunted.

Then she walked to the ladder of the diving board. The metal rungs were chilly under her bare feet, but Jessica kept her eyes on the dark night sky. Almost in no time, she was pulling herself up onto the platform.

Being up on the diving platform during the day was one thing. She had dived from it many times. But at night, in the darkness and silence, it was a completely different experience. It was scary and exciting at the same time. Her heartbeat hammered in her chest as the breeze ruffled her hair. Jessica recognized the sensation with a shock—it was almost the same feeling she had when Sam kissed her. It was a delicious, exhilarating feeling.

Slowly, Jessica walked to the end of the board. When she looked down, there was nothing to see except an occasional glimmer as a wavelet caught some starlight. She knew that when she dove there would be no way to judge how soon she would hit the water. She would meet its cold surface without warning. She paused.

71

"Two ways down, Jessica," Bruce called out. "You can always go back down the ladder."

"No way," Jessica called out. And then under her breath she added, "This is for you, Sam."

Then she quickly raised her arms over her head and dove out into the darkness.

Almost immediately, she hit the water and plunged down deep. By instinct, Jessica bent her body upward, and kicked. In a moment, she reached the surface of the water.

"Whew!" she gasped. "Fantastic!"

Ronnie knelt by the edge of the pool and held out his hand to her. "You're amazing," he said with admiration as he helped her out.

Jessica stood dripping by the edge of the pool, breathing hard and grinning from ear to ear. She felt a satisfying surge of success. Now she knew she could create the danger and control the fear. In that moment she felt that there was nothing she couldn't do.

"Totally awesome," Tad said when Jessica walked back to the fence.

In the darkness Bruce's face was impossible to read.

"Let's celebrate," Ronnie suggested.

Jessica was still smiling in triumph as she dressed and climbed back over the fence. When she landed next to Bruce, she could feel him watching her. Jessica chuckled softly. She was enjoying their escalating contest of wills very much.

"Bruce, you should never, never, never underestimate me," she told him.

"I never do," he replied in a distant voice.

She snorted. "Ha."

"Come on," Tad said. "Let's go to the Dairi Burger. I'm starved."

"You're always starved," Ronnie said, laughing.

Jessica walked back to her Jeep. Tad and Ronnie had already gotten into their cars, gunned their engines, and torn off onto the street. Bruce was waiting by his Porsche.

"You really think you can handle yourself, don't you?" he asked.

Jessica climbed into the Jeep and leaned out the open window. "Yes, Bruce, I do."

She smiled as, without a reply, Bruce got into the low-slung black sports car. The Porsche's powerful engine roared to life and took off with squealing tires. Jessica loved seeing Bruce so frustrated.

When Jessica walked into the Dairi Burger followed by the other members of Club X, her eyes were sparkling like stars. The group found an empty table and claimed it.

"Drinks all around," Ronnie said, thumping his fist on the table and tossing back his damp hair.

Jessica tossed hers in response and laughed out loud from sheer excitement.

"What have you guys been doing?" Michael Harris asked from the next table. "A little skinny-dipping, maybe?"

"We just ran under a sprinkler," Jessica said, trying to keep a straight face.

Ronnie and Tad both burst out laughing. Bruce

smiled quietly, and strolled over to the counter to order a soda.

"Come on," Michael pressed. He pulled his chair over to their table. "This has to have something to do with Club X, right?"

"That's a possibility," Ronnie said.

As the boys spoke, Jessica fingered her wet hair in thoughtful silence. She was still unsure of what Sam's reaction to Club X would be. She knew that she didn't want him to find out about her involvement from anyone but her. And Michael was Sam's good friend. It would be natural for him to mention the club to Sam the first chance he got. Like as soon as Sam returned from Colorado. But if Michael *joined* the group, Jessica thought, he would be sworn to the same oath of secrecy as the rest of them. Still, there was no point in taking chances. Once again, Jessica made a silent promise that she would tell Sam all about the club, but that first she would have to find both the perfect opportunity and just the right words. Jessica focused on the boys sitting around her and noticed Michael watching her. She sent him what she hoped was a mysterious, Mona Lisa smile.

Bruce came back with a soda, and straddled a chair. "Thinking about joining us, Harris?" he asked.

"Well, maybe," Michael said. He looked at each member of the group in turn. "What do I have to do?"

"First of all, you have to join before we tell you anything," Jessica told him.

Tad nodded and hunched his football player's

shoulders inside his black leather jacket. "That's right. You don't get to see the playbook unless you join the team."

"If all I have to do is run under a sprinkler, I think I can handle it," Michael said.

"Oh, that's just a little purification ritual," Jessica teased.

Ronnie grinned at her and wiped a wet strand of hair off his cheek.

"You can join us if you want, Harris," Bruce said. "You'll have to keep up with Jessica, though. She's a real man."

"More of a man than you are, Bruce." Jessica crossed her arms and shot him a smug look.

Michael looked at Bruce and nodded. "OK," he said. "I'm in."

"Monday night," Bruce said tersely. "My house."

"You're going to have lots of fun," Jessica assured him. "I know I am."

Todd pulled his car up to the curb and switched off the engine. "Pretty stupid movie, wasn't it?" he asked, gently sweeping Elizabeth's hair back off her shoulders.

"Pretty stupid," Elizabeth agreed with a smile. She put one hand over her mouth to stifle a yawn. "Will you hate me forever if I don't ask you in? I'm exhausted."

"Sure, no problem," Todd said. "I'll call you tomorrow."

Elizabeth smiled at him gratefully and leaned

toward him to kiss him good-night. Then she climbed out of the car, headed up the walk, and let herself in the front door.

"Jess? Is that you?" Mr. Wakefield called from the den.

"It's Liz, Dad," Elizabeth replied.

Mr. Wakefield came out into the hall, yawning and rubbing his neck. "I fell asleep going over some legal briefs," he said with a tired smile. "Is Jess home yet?"

"I didn't see the Jeep," Elizabeth admitted.

"That's funny," her father said. "It's Friday night, and Jessica's studying this long with Lila? Personally, I don't believe she's cracked a single book. I think I know what's going on."

Elizabeth felt her stomach lurch. "You—do?" she asked.

"Yes." Mr. Wakefield chuckled. "Sam's away, so Jess is taking the opportunity to catch up on all the gossip. They're probably doing strange things to each other's hair, too."

"Oh, well, I doubt that," Elizabeth said vaguely.

"Anyway, I'm going to bed, sweetheart," her father said. "If you're still up when Jessica gets home, tell her that Sam called, OK? Thanks."

Elizabeth smiled as her father trod wearily up the stairs. But once he was out of sight, she tramped into the kitchen wearing a scowl. The sooner Jessica got out of Club X, the better!

Seven

After lunch on Sunday, Elizabeth went into the backyard with a book. Jessica was floating on a raft in the pool, a cool drink in her hand and designer sunglasses shading her eyes. Her body glistened with suntan oil. A tape deck sat on the picnic table, playing the latest music from one of Jessica's favorite groups.

"Time to turn over," Elizabeth called out to her sister. "You're getting well-done on that side."

Jessica dabbled one lazy foot in the water, sending her raft drifting toward the edge of the pool. "Just a few more minutes," she mumbled in a sun-drowsy voice.

Elizabeth sat in a lounge chair and opened her book. For a few moments, she read contentedly. But the music was too loud, and each time Jessica drifted in and out of her field of vision, a nagging worry resurfaced in Elizabeth's mind. She stood up and turned the volume down.

"Hey, Jess?" she asked, sitting down again.

"Mmmm?"

"How's Club X doing?"

Jessica raised her sunglasses and cast a quick look at the back door of the house.

"It's doing just fine, Liz," she replied.

Elizabeth shifted uncomfortably in her chair. "Are you going to stick with it?"

"Mmmmhmmm." Jessica had let her sunglasses fall back on her nose and had returned to her sunbaked trance.

"I just thought that maybe you'd had enough of it," Elizabeth went on casually.

"I'm not quitting, Liz," Jessica replied. "That club is a total rush."

Elizabeth bit back a facetious reply about the vital importance of a total rush. She didn't want to antagonize her sister. Elizabeth knew from long experience that Jessica was stubborn enough to do something just because she was asked not do to it.

"Well, don't do anything I wouldn't do," she said flippantly.

Jessica suddenly put her hand to her sunglasses, rolled off her float, and plunged into the water. When she came up, she hung onto the side of the pool next to Elizabeth and stared up, her eyes hidden by her wet sunglasses.

"Look, Liz," Jessica said, "I almost *always* do things you wouldn't do. In fact, sometimes it seems as if I *only* do things you wouldn't do.

78

Don't worry about me. I can handle myself. I have everything under perfect control."

Elizabeth was too irritated by Jessica's offhand tone to respond. Instead, she placed her hands on the arms of her chair and sighed.

"You just keep playing Sweet Valley High's official hostess," Jessica went on in an overly sweet and patient manner. "And I'll just keep my membership in Club X. OK?"

"No," Elizabeth said, standing up and turning toward the house. "It's not OK. But I'll stop bothering you about it."

Jessica pushed away from the wall and floated out on her back. "Thanks."

"Jess?" Elizabeth called from the door. "Did you call Sam back yesterday?"

"I tried a couple of times," Jessica answered. She lowered her sunglasses again and looked directly at Elizabeth over the rims. "He was out all day on some kind of field trip with the group."

Elizabeth shrugged as she opened the door and stepped inside.

Jessica watched Elizabeth go in the house. Elizabeth was very good at making her feel about two inches tall. And she had done it again. It was true that Sam had been out the one time Jessica had tried calling him on Saturday. After that one time, she hadn't tried again.

Now that Michael Harris was going to be a member of Club X, Jessica had decided that she would have to start laying the groundwork with

Sam. He didn't have to know everything right away—just the outlines. She was pretty sure that if Sam returned from Colorado and found out from a source other than Jessica that she had been hanging out with a gang of boys headed by Bruce Patman, he would be a bit ticked off.

With a grimace of impatience, Jessica slid off her raft again and vaulted up onto the side of the pool. The cordless phone was sitting on the table next to the tape deck. Jessica picked up the phone, turned down the volume on the tape deck, and wrapped herself in a towel before throwing herself onto a chaise longue. She quickly tapped in the phone number at Sam's dorm.

"Yeah, Sam Woodruff? He's around here someplace. Hang on," said a male voice at the other end of the line.

Jessica clicked the earpiece of her sunglasses against her front teeth while she waited. It was going to be a tricky conversation.

"Hello?" Sam said.

"Guess who, nature boy," Jessica replied in her most sultry voice.

"Michelle Pfeiffer?" he teased.

"Ha, ha. How are you?" Jessica asked. "I miss you."

"I miss you, too. What have you been doing?"

Jessica let out an airy tinkle of laughter. "Would you believe, hanging out with Bruce Patman?"

"No." Sam laughed. "Unless you're serious, in which case, maybe I have something to worry about."

"Listen, you definitely don't have anything to

worry about. I love you," Jessica said truthfully. She went on with her story, keeping her voice full of drama. "The thing is that Bruce started this club which he said only *real* men had the guts to get into, and I just *had* to prove him wrong, right?"

Sam laughed again. "Knowing you, yes."

Jessica joined him by laughing along. "Yeah, you know me. Well, listen, I hate to do this, but I have to run," she said hurriedly. "Lila just pulled up and I'm not even dressed for the mall yet!"

"OK. I should get going, too. I'll call you later. Bye."

Jessica blew a kiss into the phone. "Love you," she said before she hung up. There, she had told Sam the truth—in a manner of speaking. The fact that she had left out the critical pieces of information, such as the nature of the club itself and her personal campaign to best Bruce, well, that could all come later. He would be home soon, she reasoned. And she would explain everything then.

On Monday, two unexpected events took place. First thing in the morning, all the students whose lockers were in the second-floor west wing discovered that their locks were frozen shut. The grumpy janitor spent half an hour opening the padlocks, and it was finally discovered that the insides of the locks had been filled with glue. Then, in the afternoon, the electricity went off three times in three different parts of the school. Whispered speculations spread across the campus, and Jessica noticed several teachers eyeing her black leather jacket with suspicion.

Jessica knew without being told that both events were the work of her fellow Club X-ers. Either Ronnie or Tad or Bruce had seen an opportunity for making trouble, and had followed his daredevil instincts. Jessica almost laughed aloud the third time the power went off. As a solution to combating boredom at Sweet Valley High, Club X was really paying off.

Monday night, Jessica was back at Bruce's house. She leaned her elbows on the table, propped her chin in her hands, and stared at the roulette wheel. There were now five pie-pieces of cardboard filling the circle. Michael's name was with the others. He hadn't been given a dare yet, but he was ready, willing, and able.

"Who poured glue in the locks this morning?" Jessica asked.

Tad smiled proudly. "I did," he admitted. "That was pretty funny, wasn't it?"

"Not bad," Bruce agreed. "And nice work on the fuse boxes, Edwards."

Ronnie smiled smugly.

"So, who got the last dare on the wheel?" Michael asked.

"I did," Ronnie said. "But it almost landed on Jessica. She had the one before me."

Jessica frowned. The arrow *had* almost landed on her the last time. Until now, the odds had been one in four. Granted, it was possible to get the same result several times in a row. Jessica had not completely followed the logic of probability in math class, being occupied with more important matters at the time. But she did remember that probability dictated that in the long run, they would all end up with the same number of dares.

And now, with the odds at one in five, the arrow was even less likely to land on her name again. Jessica felt a sense of satisfaction. Carrying out a dare was fun, but she wouldn't mind letting someone else take the risks for a few turns.

"So, let's get going, here," Bruce said. "Let's see if it's going to be ladies' night again."

"Cute, Bruce," Jessica drawled. "Odds are one in five. It could be you as easily as me."

Bruce widened his eyes innocently. "Yes, I guess you're right, Jessica. It could be."

Shaking her head, Jessica reached out to spin the wheel. The names whirled by in a blur and slowly came to a halt. Jessica's name was under the arrow again.

She glanced quickly at Bruce. He seemed as surprised as everyone else.

"You again," he said. "You've got all the luck, I guess."

"Yeah, I guess," Jessica replied. It briefly crossed her mind that maybe Bruce had somehow rigged the wheel. *I'm just being paranoid*, she decided with a shrug. There was nothing but chance at work in the roulette wheel. "So what's my dare?" she asked.

Bruce reached into his back pocket and pulled

out an unopened box of cigarettes. He tossed them casually onto the table.

"I don't get it," Michael said.

"Tomorrow morning, before homeroom, Mr. Cooper's office." Bruce smiled at Jessica.

Her stomach took a dive. She stared down at the pack of cigarettes. There were stiff penalties for smoking in school. Worse, Jessica hated cigarettes. She had tried smoking before, and had found it completely disgusting. What some kids saw in cigarettes totally escaped her.

"You're not going to back out, are you?" Bruce asked as her silence continued. His mocking eyes challenged her.

"No," Jessica said, grabbing the pack. She glared at him as she stuffed it into her pocket. "I'm not backing out."

"Doesn't one of us have to go with her?" Tad asked. "To make sure she goes through with it?"

Jessica's thoughts were racing. To avoid being caught, she would have to distract the secretaries if any had already arrived, and, most importantly, get Mr. Cooper himself out of the way. He was *always* at school early.

"I'm going to need some help," she announced. "Someone needs to get Cooper out of his office before I go in. Or do I have to take care of that, too?" she asked Bruce pointedly.

Bruce smiled. "We'll help. But the bottom line is, you're the one who has to smoke in his office."

"I know," Jessica growled. "You don't have to keep reminding me."

Bruce just let out a loud, almost cheerful laugh.

He's really enjoying this, Jessica thought. *The problem is, he's enjoying it way too much.*

Jessica had worried about getting up an hour earlier on Tuesday morning. But as it turned out, she was awake even before she had to be. Waves of nervousness rippled through her from the moment she opened her eyes, and made her hands tremble slightly as she dressed. She was anxious about smoking, and even more anxious about getting caught in the act.

But that's the whole point, she reminded herself as she waited outside for Bruce to pick her up. *There's no fun without the danger.*

"Tad and Michael are meeting us there," Bruce said as he maneuvered his Porsche through the early morning traffic. "They're working on some excuse to get Chrome Dome out of the way."

"Great," Jessica muttered. She stared glumly out the window. Ordinarily, she would have enjoyed the chance to ride in Bruce's luxurious car, but this morning she was far too nervous. She felt the hard rectangular lump of the cigarette box in her jacket pocket and gulped.

"Not nervous, are you?" Bruce asked.

Jessica managed a nonchalant smile. "No way."

"Cheer up," he said with a grin. "Maybe Cooper won't be early today."

Maybe the whole school will be locked and we won't be able to get in, Jessica hoped silently.

"That wouldn't be any fun at all, Bruce," Jessica

said aloud, sinking down cozily in the leather seat. "I'd be totally disappointed."

Bruce didn't say anything more until they reached school. Tad and Michael were waiting on the front steps. "Cooper's car is here," Michael announced as Jessica and Bruce walked up to meet them.

"Great," Jessica chirped. "This is going to be fun."

"Got your plan worked out?" Bruce asked them.

Michael nodded. "Yeah. We're all set."

Tad and Michael jogged up the steps to the front door and let themselves in. Jessica and Bruce followed behind them. Jessica was still fingering the cigarette pack in her pocket when a sudden jolt ran through her.

"I forgot matches," she said.

Bruce held open the front door for her. "I didn't."

"Oh," Jessica felt her stomach sink. "Good. Good thinking."

They walked quietly down the hallway. The corridors always seemed strange to Jessica when they weren't full of students, when they weren't ringing with the sound of banging locker doors and shouts of laughter. Up ahead, light poured out of the open door of the administration office. Jessica and Bruce went in and stepped behind a tall row of filing cabinets while Michael and Tad waited to knock on Mr. Cooper's inner-office door.

Bruce leaned out, and gave Michael the signal. Instantly, Michael rapped on the office door.

"Mr. Cooper?" he called out.

There was a sound of muffled footsteps. Then the door opened. Behind the filing cabinets, Jessica closed her eyes and tried to build up her confidence. The sense of daring and excitement she had felt on Friday night wouldn't come back. All she felt about her upcoming dare was dread.

"Mr. Cooper? I hit your car in the parking lot," Michael said in an apologetic voice. "At least, I think it's your car. You'd better come take a look."

"Oh, no," Mr. Cooper said angrily. "You kids are so reckless. Let me see what's happened."

"It's not a very big dent," Tad put in.

"I didn't know these guys were such actors," Bruce said to Jessica.

Jessica's eyes widened in alarm. Bruce had barely troubled to lower his voice. What was the point of hiding if you announced to the whole world that you were hiding? Bruce met her eyes, seemed to understand her anxiety, and grinned.

One more point to you, Jessica told him silently. *But you won't see me crack again.*

Mr. Cooper, Michael, and Tad walked out of the office, shutting the door behind them.

"OK, let's get going," Bruce said, striding toward Mr. Cooper's inner office.

Jessica followed him quickly. As Bruce closed the door behind them, Jessica leaned against the edge of the principal's desk and fumbled in her pocket for the cigarettes.

"You would have to get menthols," Jessica muttered, tearing the pack open. She shook one out and put it between her lips. Bruce took a lighter from his pocket and flicked it. Jessica leaned forward, put the cigarette to the flame, and inhaled.

She immediately began to cough. Bruce smiled. With a supreme effort, Jessica stopped coughing, and drew on the cigarette again. It made her feel sick, but she refused to give Bruce the satisfaction of knowing that. She blew some smoke into the air and met Bruce's gaze steadily.

"You'd really be happy if I got caught, wouldn't you?" she asked.

"If you got caught, you'd get detention," Bruce said. "And your parents would probably ground you, too. That *would* be a shame."

Jessica drew in smoke again, fighting her growing nausea. "And then I wouldn't be able to hang out with Club X anymore, would I?"

Bruce shook his head, feigning sadness. "If you're grounded, how can you?"

Wrinkling her nose in disgust, Jessica tapped ash into the wastebasket. She would definitely be grounded if her parents found out what she was doing. A sense of cold, hard reality came over her as she dragged on the cigarette again. She wondered how she had gotten herself into such a stupid position. *Why am I doing this?* she asked herself. *What's the point?*

Jessica knew that her putting herself at risk was giving Bruce a supreme rush.

And Jessica also knew that the more dares she completed successfully, and the longer Bruce went without having to face a challenge from the wheel, the tougher she would appear to the other members of the club. He had scoffed at danger while managing to avoid it. She had scoffed at danger and stared it down. In the face of danger, she had not once cried for help. *And that's why I'm doing this*, she thought.

A smile spread across Jessica's lips as she exhaled smoke in Bruce's face. "Do I have to smoke the whole thing?" she asked. "Or have I done enough?"

"The *whole* thing," Bruce said.

Jessica shrugged, her nonchalance real, now. "Fine," she said, tapping off the ash again. "No problem."

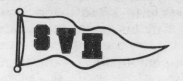

Eight

Elizabeth took her seat in homeroom and glanced at Jessica, who sat behind her. "Why did you come to school early today?" she asked.

"I had a few things to do," Jessica said distantly. She seemed to be making a point of checking over her French homework, and wouldn't look up to meet Elizabeth's eyes.

"But you got a ride from Bruce, right?" Elizabeth pressed.

Jessica shrugged, still studiously avoiding eye contact. "Yeah. So?"

"So did you come early for something to do with Club X?" Elizabeth hissed.

With her head still bent over her books, Jessica looked from one side to the other. Then she glanced up. "Not so loud, OK?"

"OK," Elizabeth whispered. "But was that why?"

Before Jessica could answer, a burst of feedback whined through the loudspeaker up on the wall. "Attention," came Mr. Cooper's voice. "A few announcements. Mr. Rizzo's first period class will have study hall, but all his other classes will meet as usual."

There was a brief silence and then Mr. Cooper continued.

"And the person who smoked a cigarette in my office this morning no doubt thinks he was being quite funny," Mr. Cooper said sharply. "If that person is also responsible for the problems we had yesterday, he is asking for serious trouble. Let me assure you, whoever you are, that you won't think you're so clever when I find you."

A few scattered laughs traveled around the room. Elizabeth felt her neck grow hot. She turned slowly and looked at Jessica, her eyebrows raised in an unspoken question.

Jessica had her chin in her hands and an untroubled smile on her lips. She arched her own eyebrows, as though surprised at Elizabeth's suspicions.

Frowning, Elizabeth turned back around in her seat and faced forward. She didn't believe in coincidences. Jessica and Bruce had come to school early, and somebody had smoked a cigarette in Mr. Cooper's office. There had to be a connection. And Elizabeth would bet money that the other recent pranks were all the work of Club X. Neither the fraternity nor the sorority pulled stunts of this nature. Pi Beta Alpha and Phi Epsilon's pranks were performed in a spirit of fun, but these had a distinct flavor of reckless arrogance and disregard for other people.

"Let me also remind you," Mr. Cooper continued, "that this Thursday our foreign guests will be returning. I would like to ask you again for your cooperation during their visit, and to warn you that if there's any funny business, the perpetrators will be punished. This school has a reputation to uphold."

"And so do I," Jessica whispered.

Elizabeth turned quickly in her seat. "What?" she asked.

"Nothing," Jessica answered. She smiled and looked back to her homework.

Elizabeth sighed in frustration. She had heard Jessica perfectly well. Jessica and the rest of Club X were not going to respect Mr. Cooper's request. Come Thursday, they would probably do something outrageous. Elizabeth hoped that somehow she could stop them.

Tuesday night found Club X gathered in the Patmans' basement again. Jessica was still glowing with her morning's success.

"Are you going to start smoking, now?" Michael teased her.

"No way," Jessica said, stretching out her legs as she leaned back on the couch. "It's a *very* dirty habit."

The boys laughed at her reference to the evidence left in Mr. Cooper's office: Jessica had left the ashes and the cigarette butt in plain view.

"Say, how did it go in the parking lot, anyway?" Bruce asked.

"My car has this dent in the rear bumper," Tad explained. "We lined up Michael's car with that, and then said we thought the Rabbit was Mr. Cooper's car."

"He was really ticked off that we thought he drove a beat-up VW," Michael said with a grin.

Tad frowned. "Yeah. I was pretty insulted."

"And I guess he didn't figure out we had anything to do with the smoker in his office," Michael went on.

"No," Ronnie said complacently. "Chrome Dome is really dumb."

Jessica regarded Ronnie silently. She *knew* that Mr. Cooper was far from dumb. He might very well have his suspicions about Michael and Tad, especially if he did some checking through the parking permit records. If he found out that the VW was registered to Tad, he might put two and two together and realize it was a ploy to get him out of the office.

But even if he worked out that much, Jessica thought, he couldn't necessarily connect Tad and Michael with her.

"Who's making up the dare tonight?" Tad asked.

"I've got a good idea," Ronnie said. He stood up and jerked his thumb toward the stairs. "Come on. I have a little demonstration to make, first."

One by one, they followed him up the stairs

93

and out the front door. Ronnie opened his car door, and lay down across the front seat.

"Watch closely," he said, his eyes twinkling with mischief. He groped under the dashboard with an expression of concentration. Then he pulled out two wires. "Observe that at no time do my hands touch the ignition. There is no key up my sleeve."

"Cool," Michael said, nodding. "You're hot-wiring it."

Jessica leaned in closer for a better view. While she watched, Ronnie touched the two wire ends together and the engine roared to life.

"Where'd you learn that?" Tad asked.

"Some guys I used to hang out with," Ronnie said carelessly. "We did it all the time."

"Let me try it," Michael requested.

Ronnie untwined the wires, and put them back in place under the dash. Then he explained and demonstrated the technique a few more times. After they were all sure they understood the procedure, they went back inside and trooped downstairs again.

"Whose car gets hot-wired, anyway?" Bruce asked as they stood around the roulette wheel.

Ronnie grinned. "What do I care? Whoever gets the dare just picks a car and drives it somewhere—say, to the Dairi Burger."

Tad and Michael both chuckled, but Jessica felt a bit sick. What Ronnie was talking about wasn't just breaking some silly school rules. He was talking about breaking the law. He was talking about stealing a car.

"Does anybody care that this is totally illegal?" she asked casually. "This qualifies as a real crime, you know. It's a bit more serious than trespassing at the pool."

"What's wrong?" Bruce asked. "Do you have a problem with that?"

"I don't if you don't," Jessica replied quickly. "I just want to make sure everyone knows what he's getting into."

Bruce gave her another wolfish grin. A lock of his dark hair had fallen across his eyes, making him look very sexy. Jessica looked away.

"I'll spin," Ronnie offered.

Jessica watched closely as the wheel spun around. But just by watching, there was no way she could tell if it was rigged. She glanced furtively at Bruce. The rapid clicks grew farther apart, and at last the wheel stopped. Jessica looked back to the wheel.

"Wait—" she gasped.

"Jessica *again*?" Bruce said.

Jessica raised her head and met his eyes. She was furious. She *knew* now, without evidence but without a doubt, that Bruce was rigging the wheel. The night that Ronnie's name had come up was a fluke: the look of surprise on Bruce's face had given him away.

Jessica was also pretty sure that Bruce alone was rigging the wheel. The other boys were in it for kicks and clearly wished they would find their own names coming up more often. And besides, they genuinely seemed to admire her. As far as Jessica could tell, none of them had any motive for wanting to drive her out of the club. All of them, except Bruce, had accepted her as one of them, had teased her about her brashness and steely nerves. No, it was all Bruce's doing.

"You don't have a problem with stealing a car, do you?" Bruce asked.

"I already told you I didn't," Jessica said through clenched teeth. Then she turned on her heel and stormed up the stairs.

"Is she quitting?" she heard Michael ask.

"Maybe," Bruce replied.

Jessica opened the front door. "See you at the Dairi Burger!" she yelled back over her shoulder.

Then she ran down the steps and yanked open the door of Bruce's car. Her heart pounding, Jessica felt under the dashboard until her fingers touched the wires. With a grin of pure delight, she pulled them out and twisted the ends together like Ronnie had shown her how to do. In a moment, the Porsche's engine started with a roar.

Jessica laughed as she sat up and pressed down the clutch. As she put the car into first gear, she saw the front door of the house bang open and Bruce dash out onto the porch.

"Wakefield!" he yelled. "Not my car!"

With a wave of her hand, Jessica let out the clutch, and the car shot down the driveway. She laughed triumphantly as she saw Bruce in the rearview mirror, running after her and waving his fist in the air.

"That's what you get, Bruce Patman," she said, turning onto the road, tires squealing.

* * *

Elizabeth glanced at her watch as Todd pulled his car into the parking lot of the Dairi Burger. Enid and Hugh were to meet them there in a few minutes.

"I think we're early," she said as she opened the car door.

"You're always early," Todd replied affectionately. "That's to make up for Jessica always being late."

"Maybe it is," Elizabeth said with a laugh. As she got out of the car, she saw the familiar black Porsche turn into the parking lot. "Here's Bruce."

"Bruce doesn't have blond hair," Todd pointed out.

Elizabeth squinted as if to better believe the strange sight that greeted her—her sister getting out of the driver's seat and slamming the door.

"Hi, Liz," Jessica said as she strolled over. On the way she stuffed her hands into the pocket of her Club X leather jacket.

"Where's our Jeep?" Elizabeth demanded. "And *what* are you doing with Bruce's car?"

"Oh," Jessica said lazily. "That. I stole it."

"Oh, come on." Elizabeth laughed nervously. "You're kidding, right?"

Jessica smiled and shook her head. "No, I'm not. I stole Bruce's Porsche and left the Jeep at his house. A fair exchange, don't you think?"

Elizabeth grabbed Jessica's arm and pulled her a few yards away among a row of cars. "This stupid club is going to get you in big trouble," she whispered angrily. "Why don't you just quit?"

"No way," Jessica said, lifting her chin stubbornly. "That's exactly what Bruce wants. And I'm not going to give it to him."

"Why not?" Elizabeth asked, throwing her hands up in frustration. "He gets everything *else* he wants! Why break a perfectly good record?"

"He's just seeing how far he can push me." Jessica said, her voice edged with fury.

"And hasn't it occurred to you that if you let him continue to push you, he'll push you right over the edge? Come on, Jess! Stop acting so childish."

"What do you mean, childish?" Jessica demanded hotly.

"Todd?" Elizabeth turned around and beckoned him over. There was no point in secrecy anymore. "Jessica, you know what happened during the last Phi Epsilon rush."

"Great, do you have to bring that up?" Todd asked with an embarrassed laugh. Then he looked carefully at the twins and saw the serious, angry expressions on their faces.

"Listen, Jessica," he said soberly. "Whatever's going on with you and Bruce is not worth the trouble. Bruce is a master of getting people to do stupid things."

"It's not worth it!" Elizabeth repeated. "Your membership would mean something if you were overcoming *real* challenges, but you're not! Bruce just keeps setting you up for a fall."

Todd nodded. "Just walk away from it, Jess. *You'll* be the winner."

"That's right," Elizabeth went on urgently. "Look, you started out to prove a case of sex discrimination, and that was OK with me. But now you're just getting carried away with this. It's become some sort of crazy personal vendetta."

"Do you know what time it is?" Jessica asked, covering her mouth to hide a yawn. "I'm expecting some people to show up any minute now."

"Jessica!" Elizabeth clenched her fists. "Please *listen* to us!"

At that moment, three cars came speeding down the street and turned to enter the Dairi Burger parking lot. Jessica leaned casually against the nearest car, hands in her pockets, and watched as they came to a stop.

Tad, Ronnie, Michael, and Bruce climbed out of the cars and slammed their doors. Bruce had ridden with Michael.

"You're too much, Jessica!" Ronnie yelled.

"You should've seen Bruce's face!" Tad cried.

Jessica pushed herself away from the car and walked over to join them. Elizabeth watched from where she stood.

"Thanks for letting me borrow your car, Bruce," Jessica said, loudly enough for her sister to hear. "It's getting a little low on gas, though. Next time, could you fill it up, first?"

The boys collapsed into appreciative laughter but Bruce's demeanor remained one of icy fury. "Nice trick, Wakefield," he said quietly. Then he nodded toward Elizabeth. "You should keep an eye on your sister, Liz. She has sticky fingers."

Elizabeth was silent. She wished she could think of the right thing to say to both Bruce and Jessica—the magic word that would bring them both back to reality.

I'll keep an eye on her, she said to herself. *You can count on that.*

Nine

Lila and Amy cornered Jessica before homeroom on Wednesday morning.

"I heard you stole Bruce's car last night," Amy said eagerly. "Did you?"

"And is he having you arrested?" Lila grinned excitedly.

Jessica hooked one finger under the collar of her jacket, and slung it over her shoulder. "Why would he do that? It was just a little joke between us."

"Ha." Lila shook her head. "Little joke. Nobody *touches* Bruce's car and lives, let alone *steals* it. He must be steamed up, big time."

"Well, actually," Jessica said, "he *is* steamed. And I love it."

Amy shrieked with laughter. "Keep it up, Jess. I *love* seeing Bruce ticked off!"

"Thanks for your support," Jessica said with heavy irony.

As Jessica walked to homeroom, she turned her thoughts to finding an opportunity for fun at school. If she could think of a very risky way in which Club X could strike, and if she could pull it off successfully . . .

As Jessica passed the administration office, she saw one of the secretaries handing a sophomore a note. "Give that to Mr. Blanchard, please," the secretary said.

The seed of an idea took shape in Jessica's mind. If all the teachers received notes to report to the principal's office at the same time . . . She smiled. Third period would be best, she decided. That was when she had math.

"This is how Club X works," Bruce said that night to the two new recruits, Charlie Cashman and Jim Sturbridge. "You screw up the dare, you get another space on the wheel and the odds against you go up. Any questions?"

Jessica was sitting by herself on a couch while Bruce explained the roulette wheel. Jessica kept her eyes on him while he talked. He hadn't looked directly at her once since she arrived. Jessica suspected that he was still furious with her—but possibly more wary of her, too. Jessica dug her hands into her jacket pockets and leaned her head back against the cushions. The discussion at the table was making her restless.

"We're going to spin twice tonight," Bruce concluded. "Just so the new guys can have a double shot."

"All right," Charlie said with a laugh.

Jessica rolled her eyes. She was not thrilled about Charlie Cashman's having joined the club. He was a bully and a loudmouth. He had already scoffed at the idea of Jessica's belonging to the group, and even Ronnie's listing of the dares she had completed didn't seem to impress him. From time to time he looked at her skeptically. Jessica tried to ignore him.

"Are you joining us?" Bruce called to her.

"I'll sit here," she replied, still contemplating the ceiling. "You don't need me standing with you for you to spin the wheel."

"Suit yourself," Bruce said.

"Hey, Jessica," Tad asked, "was it you who got all the teachers running during third period?"

"It was *you*?" Charlie asked.

"Yes, it was me," she replied in a bored voice. "How did you like my little stunt, Bruce?"

"Not very much," Bruce answered. "Fourth period would have been better for me."

Jessica shrugged. "Too bad," she said.

Bruce leaned across the table and gave the wheel's handle a twist. As the wheel spun, Jessica stared at Bruce until he raised his eyes to hers. The wheel slowed and halted. Jessica waited.

"Harris, you're up," Ronnie said, slapping Michael on the back.

Jessica, still holding Bruce's gaze, allowed herself a thin smile. She had forced him to back down! He hadn't rigged the wheel this evening! Her spirits soared. She imagined a neon sign over

the Patmans' mansion: *Jessica Can Do Anything!*
She chuckled softly.

"So what do I have to do?" Michael asked.

Tad reached into his back pocket and extracted
a piece of folded paper. "Post this list in the teachers' lounge tomorrow."

Michael unfolded the sheet and scanned it
quickly. Then he laughed out loud.

"What is it?" Ronnie asked.

" 'Hottest Babes of Sweet Valley High,' " Michael read. "Ms. Dalton is number one."

Jessica felt a wave of disgust. She had stormed
the ramparts and entered the fortress, maybe
even won the battle, but she hadn't won the war.
"That is *so* obnoxious, you guys," she
complained.

Bruce was reading over Michael's shoulder.
"What's wrong? You're number two, Wakefield."

The boys laughed appreciatively.

"Gee, this dare doesn't sound particularly dangerous to me," Jessica pointed out. "Stupid, yes.
But not quite as risky as some of the things *I've*
had to do."

"If Ms. Dalton catches him, it'll be dangerous
enough," Charlie said with a snicker.

"Come on," Jim Sturbridge said. "Let's do the
second spin."

On the second Thursday of the teacher delegation's visit, the two student-host teams traded
schedules. Elizabeth made sure she got to school
early so that she could meet the teachers as they

arrived. Just as she reached the front steps, the mini-van with the words "International Teachers' Project" lettered on the side pulled up.

"Welcome back to Sweet Valley High," Elizabeth said brightly, as Mr. Turner-Cox and Madame Erlane stepped out of the van.

"Good morning," the Englishman said in a hearty voice.

"*Bonjour*," Madame Erlane added as Mr. Srinivasen joined her on the sidewalk. He smiled and turned to admire the broad, green front lawn of the school.

"So many attractive trees," he exclaimed in his lilting accent. "Such a pleasing prospect."

A frown crossed Madame Erlane's face. "And what is the meaning of this?" she asked as she pointed her finger across the lawn.

"Meaning of what?" Elizabeth answered.

She turned to look in the direction the French woman had indicated. At first she saw nothing unusual, but then she noticed that the teachers were looking up at the trees. And then she saw what they were pointing at: From the tallest tree waved a white flag with the words "Rock 'n' Roll 4-Ever" scrawled on it in bright red paint. A wave of irritation swept through Elizabeth.

"Oh, I, uh, that's just a joke," she said as lightly as she could. *Club X,* she added to herself. *This is getting way out of control.*

Elizabeth gestured toward the steps. "Why don't I take you to the teachers' lounge now. You can have some coffee," she said.

As the group followed her, each turning at least

once to take a last look at the renegade flag, Elizabeth forced herself to chuckle. "Maybe it's an advertisement for some new tree-climbing rock group," she suggested desperately.

The visiting teachers smiled politely and followed Elizabeth up the stairs. When they got to the front door, they met Todd who was coming around from the side of the building.

"Look at that," Elizabeth whispered to him, sliding her eyes in the direction of the flag.

Todd looked and sighed. "Let me guess," he whispered back.

"Why did they have to do it *today*?" Elizabeth asked as she and Todd led the way to the teachers' lounge.

"Yeah, brilliant timing," Todd agreed.

"Right in here," Elizabeth said cheerfully as she opened the door to the lounge. "Coffee, tea, orange juice. Donuts and Danish. Help yourselves!"

The teachers filed past her into the lounge, and as Elizabeth shut the door after them, she offered a silent prayer that nothing else would happen that day. Power failures, phony emergency faculty meetings—what was next?

"Elizabeth?" asked Mrs. Vlasaya, the teacher from Russia.

Elizabeth felt a sinking sensation in her stomach. She cast a desperate glance at Todd and hurried across the room. "Yes?" she asked.

"This list," Mrs. Vlasaya said, pointing to a piece of paper that was thumbtacked to the bulletin board. "This is a list the teachers have posted?"

Elizabeth moved closer to read the sheet of paper. *"Hottest Babes of Sweet Valley High,"* she read silently.

"Of course not," she said quickly, as she ripped it down and tore it in half.

Mrs. Vlasaya nodded. "It is as I thought. A student prank, yes?"

"Well," Elizabeth said. How could she say yes? That would make two stupid pranks within ten minutes. The teachers would probably think that Sweet Valley High was on the verge of anarchy! But how could she lie?

"Well," she said again. "Yes, it's a prank."

"The discipline, it seems very light," Madame Erlane observed.

"Never would we permit this in our school," Mr. Srinivasen agreed.

Elizabeth met Todd's eyes and shook her head. If these antics didn't stop soon, the International Teachers' Project would be a disaster. So far, the only thing the delegation had seen at Sweet Valley High was chaos, rebellion, and crude humor.

Elizabeth knew it could *easily* get worse. And the most unbearable part of the whole thing was that Jessica Wakefield was right at the heart of it. Elizabeth squeezed the crumpled ball of paper tighter and tighter in her fist. It was time for a very serious talk with her sister.

Jessica stepped out of the girls' room near the cafeteria, and before she knew what was happening, she was being propelled backward into the bathroom. The door banged open and slammed into the wall.

"Hey hey hey!" Jessica yelled.

Elizabeth let go of her arm, but she continued to glare at Jessica. "Just tell me one thing," she said tightly.

Jessica massaged her arm where Elizabeth had gripped it. "What?" she asked defensively.

"Why is it that you and your *stupid* buddies have to pull these *stupid* stunts when you *know* the visiting teachers are here today?" Elizabeth demanded hotly.

"It has nothing to do with the teachers being here," Jessica replied. "And besides, I don't know what you're talking about."

Elizabeth closed her eyes for a moment, drew a deep breath, and opened them again. "Jessica," she said. "The flag, the babes list. Was it Club X, or wasn't it?"

Jessica turned away and pretended to check her makeup in one of the mirrors over the sink. Her twin didn't lose her temper very often, but when she did, it was pretty drastic—like when she had stormed out of the auditions for the soap opera. For several seconds, Jessica didn't speak. Her mind was racing, trying to come up with the words that would soothe Elizabeth.

"Listen, I never should have told you anything about Club X in the first place," she said finally, still pretending to fuss with her face. "Just forget I ever said anything at all, OK?"

"Jessica, how can you be so—so—" Elizabeth groaned.

Jessica met her sister's eyes through the mirror and smiled winningly. "Liz, *I personally* did not fly that flag, and *I personally* did not post that list in the teachers' lounge. I swear."

"This is supposed to make me feel better?" Elizabeth asked sarcastically.

Jessica shrugged. "Sure."

"It doesn't," Elizabeth replied tensely.

"Well, I can't help that," Jessica replied with a pout. "How can you blame me for something I didn't do? That's not fair at all. I expect more from you than that, Liz."

"*Don't* try turning the tables on me again, Jessica," Elizabeth replied sharply. "You think you're totally in control with this Club X thing, but you're *not,* and the worst part is that you can't even see it. It's like when you got involved with that weird cult—don't you see the connection?"

Jessica laughed and turned to face Elizabeth. "Oh, Liz. Come on! It's totally different."

"But it's *not,*" Elizabeth insisted. "Don't you see how Bruce is using you? It's ridiculous! He's got you so turned around that you're defending the posting of a list of *hot babes.*"

"Liz, try to see it my way," Jessica said patiently.

Instead of answering, Elizabeth turned on her heel and stalked out of the bathroom.

"Yikes," Jessica said with an exaggerated wince. Then she smoothed down the sleeves of her Club X jacket and looked into the mirror again.

Elizabeth was wrong. Things were totally different this time. A little while back, when she had been feeling depressed and lonely, she had become involved with the Good Friends, a group fanatically devoted to its leader, Adam Marvel. Adam and the Good Friends had made her feel needed and appreciated. And because she had wanted their approval, she had gradually adopted more and more of their ways and rules, until she had lost almost all of her own free will.

The position she was in with Club X was just the opposite of the one she had been in with the cult. Now *she* was the one calling the shots. *She* was the one in control of the danger. And she could leave it anytime she wanted to. That was the beauty of it. She was only staying with the club now because she would rather shave her head than let Bruce think he had scared her away.

Elizabeth is taking things much too seriously, as usual, Jessica decided. It *was* unfortunate that Elizabeth was being embarrassed by the pranks, but Jessica really couldn't do anything about that. It was pure chance, just the luck of the draw, the way the dice fell.

Or the way the roulette wheel spun. Jessica felt a chill scurry up her back, and she stared at herself in the mirror.

By the time Jessica got home from school that afternoon, she was feeling very uneasy. Elizabeth's words continued to echo in her mind. She didn't *feel* as if she were being manipulated by Bruce. But was she?

Pouting, Jessica wandered into the kitchen. The house was empty and quiet. Her parents were both at work, Steven was back at college, and Elizabeth had gone out with Todd.

Suddenly, Jessica felt very lonely. Hanging out with Club X had kept her busy lately, but it was no substitute for being with real friends, and it was *definitely* no substitute for being with Sam.

Without a second thought, Jessica grabbed the telephone and dialed the number of Sam's dorm. She tapped her foot impatiently while the phone at the end of the line rang, and rang, and rang.

"Ugh," she groaned as she slammed the receiver down.

For a few minutes, Jessica stared out the window.

"I need to talk to *someone*," Jessica complained aloud.

She picked up the cordless phone, opened the back door, and went out to the patio. Jessica dialed first Lila's number and then Amy's number, and got no answer at either home.

Then she thought of something else. "555-TEEN," she said out loud. She shrugged. She didn't think the teen hot line would be much good, but she was willing to give it a shot.

"Hello," said a girl's voice on the other end. "Project Youth."

"Hi," Jessica said awkwardly. "What's the routine here? Do I have to tell you my name?"

"Only if you want to. My name is Jennifer."

"OK, Jennifer," Jessica went on. "My name is—

Joanie. I have this bunch of friends, and my sister Li—I mean, Sue—thinks they're bad for me."

"What do you think, Joanie?" Jennifer asked.

Jessica shrugged. "I don't know. I mean, it's not like they can make me do something I don't want to do. So I don't see what the big deal is."

"But you trust your sister?"

"Well . . . yes. She's usually right," Jessica admitted grudgingly. "But not necessarily this time," she added.

"Maybe what you should do is write down your sister's arguments on a sheet of paper," Jennifer suggested. "And then see if you can shoot them down. If you can't, then she's probably right."

"Hmmm . . ." Jessica suddenly felt very irritable. She had hoped the teen hot line would just *tell* her what to do. A homework assignment was not what she had had in mind.

"Yeah, well, maybe I'll try that," she said. "I have to go. Bye."

"Call back anytime," Jennifer said quickly.

"Sure." Jessica hung up the phone, more confused and dissatisfied than ever.

Ten

"How is the International Teachers' Project going, Liz?" Mr. Wakefield asked at dinner on Thursday night.

"Fine." Elizabeth kept her eyes on her plate. "It's going fine."

"Have you had a chance to meet any of them, Jess?" Mrs. Wakefield asked.

Jessica pushed a pea around her plate with her fork. "They came into my French class this morning," she said.

"Speaking of French," Mrs. Wakefield continued, "I hope all this studying you've been doing with Lila lately is going to pay off."

"I think it will," Jessica said guiltily. "Studying with Lila" was her routine alibi for going to Bruce's house to spin the Club X wheel. Her parents had never brought up the subject of Bruce's exclusive club since she had first mentioned it. And she was in no hurry to remind them of its existence. She had explained her jacket away with another lie: She had bought it at the mall on a great sale.

As Jessica continued to play with her food she was struck with a disquieting revelation. Being a member of Club X was beginning to feel like a punishment. It was alienating her from her sister and Sam, and forcing her to lie to her parents. She didn't feel that she could talk to Amy and Lila about what was happening. Jessica realized that she was terribly lonely. She wished that Sam would come home. She almost wished she had never heard of Club X.

"I'm studying at home tonight," Jessica said quietly. She could sense Elizabeth looking at her questioningly.

What Elizabeth did not know was that Club X wasn't meeting again until Friday night. But Jessica was not about to bring up the subject with her sister again; she would only get another lecture. And with the way Jessica was feeling, a lecture was the *last* thing she wanted just then.

Friday night brought the first failure in Club X. Charlie Cashman, in spite of his bragging, was not able to complete his first dare. He was supposed to go into the Sweet Valley police station and tape a photograph of a baboon to the back of one of the officers. But Charlie was too well-known to the local police, and they were immediately suspicious when he walked into the station. Faced with so many police officers who mis-

114

trusted the very sight of him, Charlie lost his nerve and ran out of the station. On Saturday, when the club met in Bruce's basement, there were two spaces on the wheel bearing his name.

"Give me another shot," Charlie pleaded as he pounded his fist on the table. He looked both angry and embarrassed.

"Sorry," Bruce said with a fake note of apology in his voice. "It's all up to the wheel."

"Sure," Jessica said under her breath.

"What did you say, Wakefield?" Bruce questioned.

Jessica met his eyes and smiled innocently. "Nothing."

"What's the dare tonight?" Jim Sturbridge asked, giving the wheel a gentle push.

Jessica watched carefully as it turned slowly around. Was it her imagination, or did the wheel jerk slightly as her name clicked under the arrow? Before she could witness another revolution, Bruce reached out to stop the wheel.

"Tonight's lucky winner gets to take a walk on the wild side," Bruce said.

"I do that every day," Ronnie said with a laugh. "So what's the big risk?"

"You know that train trestle that goes over the ravine outside of town?" Bruce asked.

"What about it?" Charlie demanded.

"Whoever gets tonight's dare has to walk across it tomorrow," Bruce explained.

Jessica felt a prickle of nervousness in her fingertips. "What if a train comes along while the person is crossing?" she asked.

"I know the schedule," Bruce said confidently. "There won't be any trains tomorrow afternoon."

"Then what makes it so daring and dangerous?" Charlie asked.

A nasty light glittered in Bruce's eyes. "There could always be a change in the schedule."

Jessica looked at the group gathered around the table. Ronnie, Tad, Bruce, Jim, Michael—and Charlie, who had twice the chance of being chosen. The wheel had landed on her name so many times already. She was *convinced* that her name would not come up again. That is, not unless Bruce was interfering with the laws of chance by sabotaging the wheel in some way. And as Jessica looked at Bruce now, she felt a wave of apprehensiveness wash over her. Suddenly she *knew* the wheel was going to land on her name again.

"Let's just spin," she said hoarsely. "Get this thing over with."

Three minutes later, she was shrugging into her jacket and heading for the stairs. Her heart was pounding furiously and her pulse throbbed in her temples. She could hardly see the steps before her.

"See you tomorrow at three o'clock," Bruce called after her. "And I think you should wear sneakers. That train bridge is hard to walk on."

"Don't worry about me," Jessica called back down the stairs. "I'll be just fine."

On Sunday afternoon, Jessica drove to the edge of town. The road crossed the freight train tracks once, and Jessica shot an anxious glance down the line. The tracks stretched away to a vanishing point on one side, and snaked around a bend and into some trees in the other direction. Beyond the stand of shrubby trees was the ravine.

Jessica's stomach felt queasy. She didn't like heights. Walking across a trestle bridge would not be fun under any conditions. But with the chance that a freight train might come along at any moment . . . Jessica shivered.

She parked the car in the appointed place and then walked along the tracks into the trees until she came to a clearing. Ten yards away, the ground dropped steeply into a gorge with a trickle of stream visible at the bottom. The train tracks ran to the edge of the ravine, and then shot out across a metal and wood bridge. There was a one-hundred-foot stretch before the tracks rested on solid ground again. The intricate scaffolding of the bridge structure made a crisscross of shadows far below on the rocks.

Jessica observed all of this from the edge of the gorge. Suddenly, she realized that she wasn't breathing, and inhaled deeply.

"Yo! Jessica!"

Jessica looked up and saw the other members of Club X on the far side of the trestle. They seemed very far away. Without speaking, she raised an arm to indicate that she was ready. Then she walked to the tracks.

A hot, oily smell rose from the gravel in the railbed, and scorched, shriveled grass crunched under Jessica's footsteps. She stepped over the first rail and planted her feet firmly on the crossties.

"Come on!" Bruce yelled, his voice faint on the wind.

Jessica looked ahead. At the far end of the bridge, one gnarled pine tree stood out from the others, two of its twisted branches seeming to reach out for her. She fixed her eyes on those branches and reminded herself not to look down.

Arms out at her sides for balance, Jessica stepped on to the next tie. Three more steps took her out over the lip of the ravine, and a hot draft blew up between the ties. Jessica kept her eyes straight ahead.

Bruce had sworn that there wasn't supposed to be a freight train for hours. But Bruce wanted her out of the club. Jessica knew that she was a fool to trust him about something as important as the train schedule.

What am I doing here? she asked herself now. *Am I completely crazy?*

"Are you coming?" Bruce yelled.

Jessica stared across at him. Part of her badly wanted to turn and walk back to the safety of the bluff. But the stronger part of her nature wouldn't let her back down. *Yes, I am completely crazy*, she thought.

Her shadow jumped from tie to tie alongside her. A crow flew lazily under the bridge, its rough cry sounding from below Jessica's feet.

Jessica forced herself to breathe evenly. Because the ties were evenly spaced, she found herself

118

getting into a rhythm quickly. She began to walk a bit faster. She was already halfway across.

And then the rails on either side began to hum. Jessica stopped, startled. As she looked down at the shining metal, the bridge began to vibrate very slightly. Jessica's heart stopped in her chest, and then began to race madly. A train was coming.

Without looking back, Jessica began to hurry across the remaining ties, her eyes riveted now on the lone pine tree. She couldn't look at the boys. She was afraid of what she might see in their eyes.

"Jessica!" Michael shouted. "Hurry up!"

"A train's coming!" Ronnie yelled.

The bridge was trembling more strongly now, and Jessica could hear a distant rumble. Breathing hard, she quickened her pace. She was only twenty feet from the end.

And then her foot slipped. Jessica lunged forward. She fell on one knee on the ties, and found herself staring down the rest of the distance at Bruce. His face was ashen.

"Get up!" Jim yelled. He was pointing at the far side of the ravine, his eyes wide. "Get up!"

When the train trestle lurched violently, Jessica knew that the train was on the bridge. She pulled herself forward and began jumping three ties at a time. Her heart was hammering so loudly in her ears that she could no longer hear the boys shouting, although she could see their mouths moving. At last, the sloping side of the ravine came up to

119

meet her, and she jumped off the train trestle to the ground five feet below.

Its whistle blew loudly as the train clattered by. Jessica looked up and saw the frightened face of the conductor who had obviously noticed her on the tracks ahead of his monstrous train. Then his face was gone, and the cars were rumbling by, separating her from the other members of Club X, who were on the other side of the tracks.

I'm insane, Jessica thought with a shock, as if cold water had splashed her face. *This is the stupidest thing I've ever done, and I let Bruce Patman talk me into it.*

Jessica stood up and wiped the dirt from her trembling hands. Elizabeth had been right. There was no honor in taking dangerous risks. There was only incredible stupidity.

I quit, she said to herself as the last freight car rumbled past. *That is it.*

"Jessica!" came a triumphant shout.

The boys clambered up onto the trestle above her, and stood looking down with wide, excited smiles.

"That was awesome!" Tad said.

"You're a trip, Jessica," Michael added, reaching out a hand to help her climb up the bank.

Jessica managed to fake a smile, but she stood as if completely detached from the others, listening vaguely as they congratulated her on her "bravery," her "incredible nerve." Two weeks ago she would have felt a rush of victory at their praise, but now all she felt was disgust. She had had her fill of Club X.

*　　*　　*

Elizabeth was cleaning her room when the phone rang. She turned her radio down a notch and picked up the receiver. "Hello."

"Jess? Liz?" It was Sam.

"It's Liz, Sam," she said. "Jessica isn't home."

"Do you know what she's up to?" he asked. Elizabeth thought he sounded disappointed.

She searched her mind for some way to answer him without giving Jessica away. She was sure her sister was with the other members of Club X, but she had promised not to tell Sam anything about Jessica and the club before Jessica herself had had time to explain it all to him.

"Actually, I don't know where she is," she finally said. "But I'll have her call you when she gets in, OK?"

Sam sighed. "OK. Thanks, Liz. Bye."

"Bye, Sam," she answered. As she hung up the telephone, she heard a car door slam. A few moments later, Jessica came into her room without knocking.

"Listen, Jess," Elizabeth began angrily, "I just had to lie to Sam and—" She broke off as she took in Jessica's pale face and wide eyes.

"What happened?" she whispered.

Jessica pressed one hand over her mouth, and looked up at the ceiling. Finally, she took her hand away and lowered her eyes. "Nothing," she said.

"Nothing?" Elizabeth crossed the room and took Jessica's arm. "You come in here looking like

121

you just saw a ghost, and you tell me *nothing happened*?"

Jessica stepped away from Elizabeth and shook her head. "I'm telling you, nothing happened," she said firmly. "I'm perfectly fine."

"Why shouldn't you be fine, unless something happened—or almost happened? Jess, quit Club X," Elizabeth begged. "Please."

"I will," Jessica said quietly.

"You will?" Elizabeth repeated.

Jessica walked to the bathroom door, stopped, and dragged one trembling hand through her touseled hair. "Yes, I will."

"That's great, Jess." Elizabeth had never felt more relieved. "I'm really glad to hear it."

Jessica closed the bathroom door behind her, leaned her arms on the sink, and stared into the mirror for a moment. Then she splashed water onto her face and went into her room.

She dragged her phone out from under the bed by its cord and dialed the number at Sam's dorm. It rang twice, and then Sam answered.

"Hi," she said, surprised to find tears come to her eyes at the sound of his voice.

"I just tried calling you," he said. "Where've you been?"

"Out," Jessica whispered. "I had a few things to do."

She kept her eyes on the picture of Sam that she had thumbtacked on the wall over her desk. How could she have been such a fool? Why had

122

she ever tried to impress someone like Bruce? The only people whose approval really mattered were her family's and Sam's. They would never have asked her to risk her life for a pat on the back and a leather jacket.

"I miss you," she said to Sam in a choked voice. "I wish you would come back."

"I miss you, too," he replied tenderly.

Jessica suppressed a sniffle, and twined the phone cord around her finger. "I can't wait for you to come home," she said. "I have a lot to tell you."

By Sunday night, Jessica had begun to feel much better. The trembling in her hands had disappeared, and her breathing was steady and even. And as the fear evaporated, a new sensation began to take its place. A cold, hard lump of anger began to grow in the pit of her stomach. *Bruce has a lot to answer for*, Jessica realized with mounting fury. And it was time he got a taste of his own medicine.

I will quit, she told herself. *But not until I get even with Bruce.*

Eleven

For the first part of the week Jessica bided her time. When Bruce notified her of a Club X meeting, she told him she had an important social studies project due soon, and that she had to stay home to work on it. If he thought it was unusual for her to be concerned about homework, he didn't say so.

Meanwhile, as Jessica waited for the perfect opportunity to get her revenge on Bruce, the simpler, unassigned pranks continued at school. Mr. Cooper and many of the teachers were giving anyone in a black leather jacket very hard looks. Nothing could be proved against any of the members of Club X, however, because no one had been caught in the act of committing any of the pranks.

By Wednesday afternoon, Jessica had devised her plan. There was an assembly scheduled for the next day to honor the delegation of foreign teachers. It would be the perfect setting for a classic Club X episode.

"Are we spinning the wheel tonight?" she asked Bruce when she saw him in the hall.

"Eight o'clock," Bruce replied. He looked at her suspiciously and his blue eyes glinted. "Finished your project?"

Jessica smiled. Inside she felt disgust as she looked at him, but on the outside, she was as cheerful and casual as ever. "All done," she said. "Now it's time to have fun."

"Great," he said. "See you tonight."

"Time to have fun," she repeated in a low voice as Bruce walked away down the hall.

Jessica did not arrive at Bruce's until eight-twenty that night. She wanted to be sure that all of the guys were there ahead of her. Her plan depended on not having anyone else arrive after she did.

She trotted down the steps to the basement, an anxious, concerned look on her face. "Hey, Bruce. What happened to your car?" she asked.

"What?" Bruce whipped around to stare at her. "What are you talking about?"

"That crack in the windshield," Jessica explained. Thank goodness for her week-long soap opera career! That one short stint had taught her a lot about delivering dramatic news.

The boys exchanged horrified looks. Bruce's

Porsche was the most envied vehicle at Sweet Valley High.

"Get out of the way," Bruce said roughly, pushing past Jessica and hurrying up the stairs.

Just as Jessica had anticipated, all of the other boys rushed out to look, too. The moment they were gone, Jessica raced across to the roulette wheel and flicked on the overhead lamp. With her fingernail, she pried up the cardboard wedge with her name on it. Then she caught her breath. A wide, flat magnet was underneath.

Undoubtedly, there was another magnet under the arrow, but Jessica knew she didn't have much time to examine the wheel. As soon as the boys discovered that Bruce's precious Porsche was unscathed, they would be back.

Jessica hurriedly removed the magnet, peeled back the cardboard with Bruce's name printed on it, slipped the magnet underneath, and then pressed everything back into place. When Jessica switched the lamp off, she knew her adjustments would be undetectable. At least she hoped they would be. If she was caught at this stage of the game, it would be her word against Bruce's that she hadn't been the one to plant the magnet in the first place.

"Bruce, you pig," she muttered. "Let's see how you like games of chance, now."

Jessica ran lightly up the stairs and out the front door. Bruce and the other boys were still scrutinizing every inch of the black Porsche's windshield.

"What were you talking about?" Bruce asked

irritably when she strolled across the driveway to join them. "I don't see anything wrong."

"There isn't a scratch on it," Michael agreed.

Jessica stuck her hands in the pockets of her jacket and shrugged. "Wow, that's weird," Jessica said in her most innocent, bewildered voice. "Maybe it was some kind of trick of the light. The sun was just going down behind those trees when I got here."

"That could be it," Tad said, nodding sagely.

"Sorry I gave you all such massive coronaries," Jessica apologized.

"Let's go back in," Ronnie said.

"Listen," Jessica said as they all walked up the steps to the Patman mansion. "I want to make the dare tonight. I thought of a really good one."

"Something you'd be willing to do if you get stuck with it?" Bruce asked coldly.

"Oh, Bruce," Jessica said, shaking her head. "I can't believe my name will come up *again*. That would be too much of a coincidence."

"That's the weird thing about chance," Bruce said, the corner of his mouth twitching as if he were trying to hide a smile. "You just never know."

Jessica pretended to sigh. "Well, I will admit, I wouldn't mind if someone *else* had to take the dare for a change."

"Let's just spin the wheel," Charlie said.

The group trooped down the stairs to the basement, and Bruce switched on the lamp that hung over the roulette wheel. Jessica's eyes instantly looked for any sign that it had been disturbed. If

Bruce detected her switch, her plan was blown. But she could see nothing unusual, and Bruce hardly even glanced at it. It was clear that he was completely confident in his rigged wheel.

"So, we're all agreed. Whoever lands on the arrow performs Jessica's dare, right?" Bruce asked.

"Sure, fine," the others all agreed.

"I'll spin it tonight, OK?" Jessica asked. "It's landed on my name so many times that I just *know* my luck's about to turn."

Bruce held up both hands and grinned. "Well, they say luck is a lady . . ."

"Thanks." Trying not to smile, Jessica gave the wheel a sharp twist. The rapid-fire clicks buzzed loudly in the silent basement. Everyone except Jessica and Bruce watched the wheel. They watched each other.

As the wheel slowed to a stop, Jessica kept her eyes on Bruce.

"And it's the Brewster," Jim crowed.

"What?" Bruce blinked and turned to look at the wheel. An expression of utter astonishment crossed his face.

"Why so surprised, Bruce?" Jessica asked. "You didn't think it could possibly land on me *again*, did you?"

"Yeah, Bruce," Tad put in. "It has to land on you sometimes."

Bruce's throat worked as he swallowed. "Well, I know. I just—"

Jessica's eyes sparkled with her success. This was a *real* rush! Bruce couldn't explain to the others why he was so surprised. He would have to tell them the wheel had always been rigged against Jessica, and considering the fact that they all thought she was so cool, they wouldn't exactly be on his side.

"So what does he have to do?" Charlie asked.

"OK, tomorrow there's an assembly," Jessica said.

Bruce folded his arms across his chest. "Yeah. Go on. I'm listening."

"Well, I think it would be a real kick if you took a radio to school and hooked it up to the PA system to play KZZP during the assembly."

Michael laughed. KZZP was the hardest hard-rock radio station in the valley. Parents were always trying to organize boycotts of the station, and Mr. Cooper was well-known to have a vendetta against it. Students were forbidden to play KZZP anywhere on school grounds.

"Beautiful," Ronnie said. He punched Bruce in the arm. "And I guess we don't have to go with you, right? We'll all know if you did it or not."

Bruce scowled at Ronnie. "Yeah, I guess you will," he replied.

Jessica folded her arms across her chest and smiled. If she were lucky, Bruce would fail in his attempt; if she were *really* lucky, he would even get caught. But whether Bruce backed down or was caught, Jessica would announce that she was quitting the club because it was made up of a bunch of losers.

And if by any chance Bruce should succeed, she

would *still* drop out of the club. She couldn't care less what they thought of her, now.

As the members of Club X headed upstairs a while later to drive home, Jessica was stopped short by a worry she had not previously considered. The object of tomorrow's assembly was to pay respect to the visiting teachers; obviously its success would mean a lot to Elizabeth. And if Jessica had a hand in ruining the ceremony, Elizabeth would take it pretty hard.

But there's no other way, Jessica insisted to herself stubbornly. She really didn't want to hurt Elizabeth, but she just *had* to get her revenge on Bruce.

Twelve

Elizabeth drove to school the next day while Jessica finished putting on her makeup in the passenger seat. The radio was blaring KZZP, which Elizabeth hated, but Jessica had insisted on listening to it. A screaming electric-guitar riff made Elizabeth's ears ring.

"This is awful," Elizabeth said, turning down the volume.

"No, no, I like this song," Jessica said, smiling mysteriously as she rummaged in her makeup bag.

"How can you do that in a moving car?" Elizabeth asked, glancing at her twin sister as she carefully brushed mascara onto her lashes.

Jessica widened her eyes to let the mascara dry. "Easy. Just don't hit any bumps, OK?"

"Sure," Elizabeth said. She drove in silence for a moment. Then she glanced at the black leather jacket draped over the back of the passenger seat. "So, I guess you're keeping the jacket, even though you quit the club."

"I'm still in the club," Jessica replied, uncapping her lip gloss and pouting at the mirror.

Elizabeth switched the radio off. "I thought you were quitting. You *said* you were quitting."

"I am. After today." Jessica rubbed her lips together and smiled into the mirror.

"Why after today?" Elizabeth asked. "What happens today?"

Jessica popped her lip gloss back in her bag. "Nothing you need to worry about, Liz. But believe me, I'm getting back at Bruce in a *big* way."

"Jessica, there isn't going to be another stupid prank today, is there?" Elizabeth asked uneasily. "Mr. Cooper is still steaming over the last ones."

"I'm not worried about Chrome Dome," Jessica replied breezily. She turned the radio back on, and began to sing.

Elizabeth frowned. "Jessica, what are you planning? Today's the last day the teachers' delegation will be at Sweet Valley High. Please don't ruin it. I mean it."

"What are you going to do, tell on me?" her sister teased gently. Jessica's hair whipped around in the draft from the open windows, and she smiled at Elizabeth disarmingly.

Elizabeth ignored her sister and concentrated on crossing the traffic to get into Sweet Valley High's parking lot. She never deliberately got anyone into trouble, especially her own sister. But considering the kind of petty—and not so petty—

annoyances Club X had been causing lately, she was feeling pretty tempted to cause some trouble of her own!

"Listen," she said, raising her voice over the music, "you know I'm not going to turn you in, Jess. But if you spoil things today, I'm not just going to say it's OK."

"Of course you will, Liz," Jessica said, smiling sweetly. Then she let out a genuine laugh and put one arm across Elizabeth's shoulders to hug her lightly. "Come on. You *always* forgive me."

Elizabeth rolled her eyes at her sister. Sometimes, Jessica could be the most infuriating, maddening person. *But I do always forgive her*, she told herself ruefully.

"Just don't do anything we'll both be very sorry about," Elizabeth warned as she parked the Jeep. "Or I might just decide to play hardball, too."

Jessica laughed and climbed out of the car. "OK, Liz. See you later."

Suppressing a sigh, Elizabeth climbed out and slammed her door. Sixteen years of living with Jessica hadn't made the job of being her sister any easier. She knew Jessica was planning something, but she didn't know what, or how to stop it.

She was still deep in thought as she passed by the administration office, and was almost out of earshot when she heard her name called. She backtracked to the open door, and saw one of the secretaries waving at her.

"Mr. Cooper would like to see you, Elizabeth," the woman said.

Elizabeth erased the scowl from her face and went in to knock on the principal's door.

"Liz," he said, beckoning her in. "Just the person I wanted to see. Take a seat."

"What can I do for you, Mr. Cooper?" she asked, trying not to think about Jessica and Club X.

He leaned on his arms and gave her a fatherly smile. "Elizabeth, you've been terrific with our guests these past couple of weeks."

"Thanks," she said.

"And since you and the other students have really been at the heart of things while they've been here," he went on, "I want you to take a major role during our assembly this afternoon."

Elizabeth smiled, ignoring the thump of nervous apprehension she felt. "Thanks. It's been a really interesting experience."

"I want you to be the one to introduce the visiting teachers," he explained. "Everybody has seen them around campus, of course, and lots of the students have met them, but I want formal, individual introductions to wrap things up. I was going to do it myself, but then I decided this morning that it would be much nicer if you spoke a few words. I know it's short notice, but are you willing?"

"Mr. Cooper, I'm honored," Elizabeth said, trying to sound more confident than she felt at that moment. She could never tell him that she had a bad feeling about the afternoon assembly. Without proof he would never believe her. And if she shared her suspicions with the principal, she would have to give her sister away.

Mr. Cooper stood up and gave her a warm, appreciative smile. "Terrific. Just say a few words, something to sum up the experience. You'll think of something."

"I'll try," she said.

"I knew I could count on you, Elizabeth." Mr. Cooper walked her to the door and waved her out.

And I know I can count on Jessica, Elizabeth said to herself as she left the office. She shook her head wearily. *I can count on her to have absolutely perfect—perfectly terrible—timing.*

Jessica watched the clock closely after lunch was over, tapping her fingers impatiently on her desk. The suspense was almost unbearable. She couldn't wait to see if Bruce would really have the nerve to go through with his dare.

I know he'll chicken out, she thought optimistically. *I know he'll make a total fool of himself.*

And if by any bizarre chance, he *did* go through with it, he was sure to be caught. That would be almost as delicious as having him back out at the last minute!

Finally, it was time for the assembly. Jessica hummed to herself as she joined the throng pressing into the auditorium.

"Hi," she said as she found a seat next to Elizabeth. She scanned the crowd for a sight of Bruce and the other Club X members. Michael had volunteered to help Bruce by running interference with anyone who might be in the way.

Elizabeth was reading over a sheet of paper, and brushing her hair at the same time. She hardly looked up as Jessica sat down beside her.

"What's that?" Jessica asked, glancing at the page. "Getting a head start on tonight's homework?"

"It's my speech," Elizabeth replied in a preoccupied voice. "I had to write it fast. I didn't know until this morning that I was going to be part of the assembly."

"Part of the assembly?" Jessica echoed.

"That's right. To introduce the teachers, explain what they've been doing, that sort of thing," Elizabeth said.

"Part of *this* assembly?" Jessica asked.

Elizabeth stopped brushing her hair to look at Jessica. "Yes, this assembly. Which one did you think?"

"Oh . . . I don't know." Jessica turned her head away and fiddled with the zipper of her jacket.

"I hope nothing *unexpected* is going to happen," Elizabeth added meaningfully.

"Unexpected?" Jessica repeated in a hollow voice. She suddenly felt terrible. If Bruce actually went through with his dare, it could easily happen while Elizabeth was onstage. Getting her revenge on Bruce would also mean humiliating her sister in front of all of Sweet Valley High.

While she had been swept up in the early excitement of the club, Jessica hadn't cared that their pranks made Sweet Valley High look like a chaotic and undisciplined place in the eyes of their guests. But now, having been badly hurt by their antics herself, and with her sister facing the possibility of public embarrassment, Jessica found that she *did* care about the club's thoughtless behavior.

Swallowing hard, Jessica cast another nervous glance around the auditorium. This time she saw Bruce and Michael sitting in the back row, next to one of the doors. As she watched, Bruce stood up and let himself out.

Jessica stood up.

"What's wrong?" Elizabeth asked.

"I—uh . . ." *Oh, why didn't I just quit after I nearly got hit by that train?* she asked herself desperately. *Why do I always get so carried away?*

Maybe it was possible to reschedule Bruce's dare, Jessica thought. Maybe she could have it both ways—make Bruce go through with his prank, but also let Elizabeth give her speech without interruption.

"What's wrong?" Elizabeth asked again.

"I—I have to go to the bathroom," Jessica said quickly, beginning to edge out of the row.

Elizabeth reached out and grabbed Jessica's arm. "Jess—what's going to happen?"

"Nothing," Jessica said, pulling her arm away and hurrying into the aisle. She maneuvered around a group of sophomore girls who were arguing about where to sit. "The assembly is about to start," Ms. Dalton said as Jessica brushed past her.

"I have to use the girls' room," Jessica gasped.

"Make it quick," her French teacher said.

The visiting teachers were just coming into the auditorium and beginning to walk down the aisle toward the block of seats reserved for them in the front row. Suddenly Jessica found herself face to face with the Indian teacher, Mr. Srinivasen. She stepped to the left, and he stepped to the left.

"Excuse me," she said, moving right.

"Excuse me," he repeated, moving to the right at the same time. "Oh, pardon me."

Jessica felt like screaming. Every second that ticked by brought Bruce closer to Mr. Cooper's office, closer to getting into position to blast KZZP over the loudspeakers. She had to get to him and stop him before he pulled it off. And she knew, deep down, that he *would* pull it off. His arrogant pride would never let him back down.

It will work just as well tomorrow, she thought anxiously. *Just don't do it now, Bruce. Don't do it now!*

Jessica barged past Mr. Srinivasen and continued up the aisle. *So what if he goes back to India thinking that American students are rude and pushy?* she asked herself. *It's an emergency!*

With a gasp of relief, Jessica straight-armed the swinging door and burst out into the hallway. She looked around quickly for eagle-eyed, nosy teachers, and began to run toward the office. If she was lucky, she would get to Bruce while he was still angling to get at the public-address system. Jessica skidded around a corner and ran smack into Mr. Collins.

"Whoa! Not so fast, Jessica," he said, taking her arm.

138

"Mr. Collins," she cried.

"The auditorium is in the other direction, if I remember correctly," he said.

"I, uh," Jessica said, not daring to look at him. "I have to use the ladies' room."

"And *that* is in the other direction, too," Mr. Collins said firmly.

Jessica gulped. "Well, I—"

He looked at her hard. "You weren't thinking about putting up another flag, or pulling the fire alarm, were you? Something of that kind?"

Jessica's stomach flip-flopped. She should have known people would begin to suspect who was behind the mysterious pranks. For once, her fertile imagination couldn't come up with any kind of likely excuse. "What?" she whispered.

"Nobody's been caught," Mr. Collins said. "But you're not being very discreet, are you? Those jackets make it very easy to see who's in the group."

"But—" Jessica tried unsuccessfully to free her arm. "I really have to use the ladies' room."

He smiled wryly. "You're a big girl, Jessica. You can wait. I think I'd like you to sit with me in the assembly," Mr. Collins said, turning her around and leading her back down the hall.

"But—" Jessica cast one desperate look back over her shoulder as Mr. Collins marched her along. There was no way to stop Bruce now.

Thirteen

Jessica glumly followed Mr. Collins into the auditorium and took a seat in the last row, near the exit. But if she had any hope of sneaking out, Mr. Collins took care of that. He sat right beside her.

"Not thinking of going anywhere, are you?" he asked under his breath.

"No," Jessica whispered.

Up on the stage, Mr. Cooper was addressing the assembly. "It has been our honor and privilege to have these teachers as our guests for the past couple of weeks. I know I speak for all of us when I say we've enjoyed having you."

Polite applause broke out. Jessica sank into her seat. How could she ever have doubted that Bruce would go through with the dare? she asked herself morosely. What she had set up wasn't dangerous, like the dares Bruce had assigned, and Bruce would walk over fire to protect his reputation as the leader and creator of Club X. Assuming that Bruce would back down was just one of her usual silly dreams. She felt awful.

"And now, I would like to turn the microphone over to Elizabeth Wakefield," Mr. Cooper said. "Elizabeth was one of our student hosts, and I have asked her to introduce our guests to you. Elizabeth?"

More applause filled the auditorium as Elizabeth stood up and began to make her way to the stage. Jessica closed her eyes.

Not now. Not now. Not now, she chanted silently.

"Hello," Elizabeth said into the microphone, giving the student body a friendly smile.

"Hi, Liz!" a few people shouted out. Scattered laughter rippled across the room.

Elizabeth smiled again, and opened the folded paper on which she had written her speech. She looked happy, but a bit nervous, too. "When Mr. Cooper asked me to be a part of the host group, a hundred questions went through my mind," she began.

Jessica opened her eyes and glanced warily at the public-address speakers high on the auditorium wall. So far, not a peep out of them. Maybe Bruce had run into problems, and wouldn't go through with the KZZP plan after all. She drew a hopeful breath.

"I wanted to know everything about their schools," Elizabeth was saying, "and I was afraid I would be too busy asking them questions to answer the ones they had for me."

Jessica was too nervous to pay much attention to

141

what her sister was saying. She bit her lower lip and prayed that the electricity would go off or that an earthquake would strike or that Bruce would suddenly reform into a rule-following angel.

"But I forgot that teachers are teachers, no matter what country they're from," Elizabeth continued. "They're pros at asking questions. So I—"

Then it happened. With a crash of drums and a thundering bass, the sound of heavy-metal music came blaring from the loudspeakers. Jessica's heart plunged and she let out a tiny groan.

"Oh my gosh," she whispered.

Through the noise of music blasting, students talking, and chairs scraping, Jessica could hear Mr. Cooper's voice loud and clear. "This is the last straw!" he yelled as he strode up the aisle. And when he passed Jessica's seat she heard him add, "This is unsupportable!"

Mr. Collins gave Jessica a hard look and stepped into the aisle.

"Don't even think of going anywhere, Jessica," he said angrily.

Several teachers followed Mr. Cooper and Mr. Collins out the door of the auditorium. Not heeding Mr. Collins's warning, Jessica slipped out after them with a crowd of curious students.

Jessica stopped outside the door. *Now what?* she wondered. Should she follow the crowd to Mr. Cooper's office or stay in the auditorium or simply hide in the girls' room? For a split second she toyed with the idea of cutting the rest of school and stowing away on a ship to the southern hemisphere. The possibility of being blamed for the pandemonium screamed at her urgently. If Bruce managed to get away in time, there would be no hard evidence to tie the stunt to Club X. But if he were caught—

At least I have an alibi, she thought desperately. *I was sitting with Mr. Collins when the music started, wasn't I?* Jessica gulped: Mr. Collins *knew* that she was involved.

At last, the temptation to see what was happening won out over her desire to run away. She hurried along with the crowd toward the administration office. Just as they approached the doors, the music stopped in mid-wail. There was a shout, and Mr. Rizzo came out of the office, dragging a loudly protesting Bruce by the back of his black leather jacket.

Jessica froze. This was the end of Club X, for every member. Part of her was very glad. But part of her was very afraid. Bruce would not go down without a fight.

While she watched, Mr. Cooper took Bruce's arm, marched him back into the office, and slammed the door.

"Thanks a lot," said a furious voice at Jessica's elbow.

Jessica turned, her face drained of color. "Liz, I tried—"

Before she could say anything else, Elizabeth strode away.

Elizabeth was working on some homework that afternoon when Jessica finally came home. Gritting her teeth, Elizabeth bent over her notebook, determined not to speak to her sister. But, her mind in a whirl, she simply scribbled curlicues in a pretense of serious writing.

"Liz?" There was a timid knock on her door.

Elizabeth ignored it. In spite of the fact that the assembly had been salvaged after the tumultuous interlude, she was still too hurt and angry to talk about it.

"Liz? Can I talk to you?" Jessica asked, opening her sister's door and stepping inside.

"What is it?" Elizabeth said quietly without looking up from the page.

Jessica sat on the edge of Elizabeth's bed and fingered the bedspread nervously. "I'm really, really sorry. I didn't know you were going to be giving a speech when I planned Bruce's stunt. And I tried to stop him. I really did."

"Well, you were too late," Elizabeth retorted coldly. "The assembly was a complete disaster, you know," she added, somewhat untruthfully.

"But that's not my fault!" Jessica wailed.

Elizabeth turned in her chair and glared at her sister. "Not your fault? How can you say that? It was all *your* idea."

A blush swept across Jessica's face. "Well, I know it was, but—"

"How could you be so selfish?" Elizabeth demanded. "Today's assembly—the entire visiting teachers' program—meant so much to Mr. Cooper and to the teachers! And, to *me*, whom you succeeded in embarrassing. But naturally you didn't even *think* about anyone else."

"I *did*, but I honestly thought Bruce wouldn't actually go through with the stunt." Jessica sniffed and shook her head. "I'm sorry, Liz. I must be the worst person in the whole world. I bet you hate me now."

Here it comes, Elizabeth thought. *The pity act.* That was the way it had been for sixteen years. And for sixteen years, Elizabeth had forgiven her sister for everything.

"Do you hate me?" Jessica asked.

"I don't hate you, Jess," Elizabeth said. She threw her pen down on the desk and shoved her chair back. "But sometimes I really think I could kill you."

Jessica sniffed again, and managed to give Elizabeth a watery smile. "But you won't, Liz. What would you do without me?"

Elizabeth let out a short, rueful laugh. "I'd probably lead a perfectly normal life, that's what."

"And that would be pretty boring, wouldn't it?" Jessica asked hopefully.

"Sometimes I think boring would be pretty nice," Elizabeth said, crossing to the bed and sitting down next to Jessica.

Jessica wiped the tears from her cheeks and gave Elizabeth a fierce hug. "Liz, I promise, I won't ever do anything like this again. No more Club X's, no more competing with jerks like Bruce, no more embarrassing you."

As Elizabeth returned Jessica's hug, she rolled her eyes. "Do me a favor, Jess? Don't make any promises you can't keep."

Fourteen

Jessica delayed as long as possible the next morning before entering the school building. While she skulked in the parking lot, leaning against the Jeep and pretending to read her English book, she noticed that Bruce's car wasn't there. At that moment she would have given anything to know what had happened yesterday after Bruce had been caught.

Finally, Jessica had no choice but to go in or be late for homeroom and marked absent. As soon as she walked through the door of the building, however, she was greeted by a messenger from the office. He waved a pink slip at her.

"I was just going to your homeroom to find you," he said. "Your presence is requested in the principal's office."

Jessica silently took the pink slip and hurried past him.

"Oh, help," she whispered, stopping for a moment in the middle of the corridor.

There was no doubt in her mind that the members of Club X were about to meet their doom. Just how serious it was remained to be seen. As she hurried down the hallway, she passed Bruce Patman's homeroom. She could see him sitting slouched in his seat at the back of the room, looking as grouchy as a bear woken up from winter hibernation.

Jessica stopped and tried to attract his attention by waving the pink slip. Bruce glanced up, saw her in the doorway, and looked away with a sullen expression.

"Bruce!" Jessica whispered hoarsely. When he refused to turn back to her she tried again, more urgently. "Bruce!"

Bruce's homeroom teacher walked to the door, looked questioningly at Jessica, and then shut the door firmly in her face.

Groaning, Jessica turned and continued on her way down the hall. When she reached the administration office she handed over the pink slip to the secretary.

"Go right in, Miss Wakefield," the secretary said crisply.

Jessica grimaced. Sarcastic politeness in secretaries was not a good sign. She forced herself to give a wintry smile. "Thanks."

Jessica opened the door of Mr. Cooper's office and slipped inside. Tad, Ronnie, Michael, Charlie, and Jim were all there, each exhibiting various degrees of shame, humiliation, even defiance. *Well, the gang's all here*, Jessica noted to herself.

"So, you've decided to join us, Jessica," Mr. Cooper said.

"Sorry I'm late," Jessica said. The boys had taken all of the available seats; Jessica stood by the door, shifting nervously from foot to foot.

"I'm sure you have a very good idea what you're all doing here," Mr. Cooper said. "Your good friend Bruce Patman gave me your names."

"What a lousy—" Jim exploded.

"He turned us in?" Jessica asked, her voice rising in a squeak. "But we didn't have anything to do with the music coming over the PA system, Mr. Cooper."

The principal folded his arms. "No? But you all had something to do with the other juvenile, idiotic pranks that have been going on around here." Mr. Cooper picked up a piece of paper that had been lying on his desk. "Smoking in my office, flying objectionable flags, offending the female teachers on our faculty, tampering with locks, sending false messages."

"Missed a couple," Tad muttered.

"*Not* to mention setting off the fire alarms," Mr. Cooper added. "Which, I might add, is not only disruptive, but illegal!"

Jessica's cheeks were burning. She felt horrible. And she couldn't believe that Bruce had turned traitor!

"Now," Mr. Cooper continued, more calmly. "I've already dealt with Bruce. Being the ringleader of this disreputable mob has gotten him

148

two weeks' detention. And for going along with his harebrained idea of fun, the rest of you have detention for one week."

Jessica leaned back against the door. This meant no after-school activities of any kind: no cheerleading practice, no trips to the beach, no shopping, nothing. It meant sitting in study hall after school and doing homework until five o'clock. To Jessica, detention sounded worse than capital punishment.

And she didn't know *what* she was going to tell her parents, either. They were bound to notice her coming home at five-thirty every afternoon for a week. *Maybe I can tell them I'm working on an important class project,* she hazarded wildly. *Or that Lila and I have more French studying to do . . .*

"I'll be calling all your parents today, too," Mr. Cooper added.

Jessica's eyes widened. "Do you have to?"

"I certainly do," Mr. Cooper said. "I think your parents have a right to know what you've been doing with your spare time, lately."

"Great," Charlie muttered. "My old man will probably kick me out."

"That's for you and your family to work out," Mr. Cooper said. "Now that's all I have to say. It's time for first period."

One by one, the former daredevils of Club X trooped out of Mr. Cooper's office.

"Patman really stinks," Ronnie said.

"Yeah, what a bum," Tad said.

Jessica hung her head and shoved her hands in her pockets. Bruce *had* turned her in, but she had joined the club willingly. He hadn't forced her, not really. And then she had gone ahead and *stayed* in the club after she had realized how ridiculous it was. She really had no one to blame but herself.

When Jessica reported to detention that afternoon, Bruce was sitting by himself at a desk in the last row, tapping his pencil eraser on the desk and watching the clock.

"I heard his folks grounded him for a week," Michael whispered to her. "No car."

Jessica smiled bitterly. She couldn't wait to find out how her parents were going to react. She had already been grounded once recently, for having let her math grade go into a nose dive. Her parents were not going to be very pleased to hear that she had gotten into trouble again so soon. All she could do now was hope that they would remember the wild days of their own youth, and go easy on her. If they had ever *had* any wild days!

Jessica found out exactly how her parents felt at dinnertime that night.

"No driving privileges, no telephone, no friends over, and no excursions to any place except school," Mrs. Wakefield said, her eyes flashing.

"For how long?" Jessica whispered.

"A week," her father said.

"But Sam's coming home tonight," Jessica said, tears springing to her eyes.

Mrs. Wakefield frowned. "Sorry. You'll just have to wait until next week to see him."

Elizabeth smiled at Jessica sympathetically. Jessica found it impossible to swallow another bite of her dinner.

"May I be excused?" she asked quietly.

"Yes," Mr. Wakefield said.

Holding back the tears, Jessica raced up to her room and slammed the door. In all fairness, she knew that she had gotten off easily. She was surprised that her parents hadn't been more harsh with her.

But it was painful to know she wouldn't be able to see Sam, or even to talk to him on the phone. More than ever, she wished he didn't attend a different school. Just thinking about him made the tears start to fall at last.

"Oh, Liz!" she moaned, hearing footsteps in her sister's room. She ran through the bathroom and flung the door open. "You have to help me. Please. I'm *begging* you!"

Elizabeth whirled around in surprise. "What's wrong? You sound desperate!"

"I am," Jessica wailed. "Can you do me the biggest, most enormous favor any sister ever did in the history of time?"

"Well . . ." Elizabeth began.

"Sam's coming home tonight," Jessica whispered, casting a frantic look toward the door. "Switch with me just for a few minutes, *please*? I have to see him and explain things. Please!"

"Jess, I can't fool Mom and Dad into thinking I'm you," Elizabeth said.

Jessica grabbed her sister's hand. "Yes, you *can*," Jessica said. "You know you can. Do it for

151

me, please? How would you feel if you couldn't see Todd, and couldn't even tell him why? It's not me I'm worried about, but it just isn't fair to Sam, don't you see?"

"Well . . . " Elizabeth sighed and bit her lip.

"I have to see him, Liz. Please understand," Jessica pleaded.

Elizabeth shook her head. "I know I'm going to be sorry—and don't you dare ask me to do it again, because I don't want to be grounded, too—but OK. I'll do it—just this once."

"Oh, Liz, you're the best!" Jessica cried. "Call him now and ask him to meet me at the Dairi Burger, OK?"

Even as she spoke, Jessica was beginning to undress. Once she had switched outfits with Elizabeth, taken off some makeup, and put her hair in a barrette, she could walk out of the house as Elizabeth, and her parents would simply blow her a kiss goodbye.

Just before eight o'clock, Jessica arrived at the Dairi Burger, dressed as Elizabeth. She scanned the crowd quickly, and spotted him.

"Sam!" Jessica shoved her way through the crowd at the front of the restaurant.

"Jess—Liz—" Sam stood up quickly. Jessica could feel several pairs of curious eyes watching them, no doubt wondering exactly *whose* reunion they were witnessing.

Jessica reached Sam and looked up into his face, her eyes shining with happiness. She could

152

hardly keep from kissing him right there in front of everyone. Every detail of his face seemed beautiful to her. She wanted to memorize each one, and save the memories for her week of exile.

"Come outside," she said loudly. "I have a message for you from Jessica."

Sam followed her back through the crowd. As soon as they were outside and in a shadowy part of the parking lot, they stopped. Jessica's heart was pounding, and she felt an excitement more meaningful and important and valuable than anything she had felt while performing dares with Club X.

"So what's the message from Jessica?" Sam asked softly.

"This." Jessica flung her arms around his neck and kissed him on the lips. She sighed as his arms came around her and held her tight.

"OK. What's this all about, Jess?" Sam asked, pulling away after a long, quiet interlude. "Why are you grounded?

Jessica sighed again. "Sam, have I got a lot to tell you," she said. "But before I explain, I just want to tell you one thing. You're all the excitement I need, so stick around, OK?"

"What?" Sam laughed.

"Stick around," Jessica said again, giving him another lingering kiss. "It's a long, long story."

"So, how did it go with Sam?" Elizabeth asked when Jessica snuck into her sister's room at about midnight. "I hope it was spectacular. I'd hate to think I spent an entire evening hiding out from Mom and Dad, ready to pretend I was you, for nothing!"

Jessica plopped down on Elizabeth's bed and sighed. "You know, Liz, sometimes I think I'm the luckiest person alive."

Elizabeth smiled indulgently. "You *are* the luckiest person alive, Jess. How many people have sisters as wonderful as I am? And boyfriends as understanding as Sam. He *was* understanding, wasn't he?"

"Oh, yeah," Jessica said. "He was great. He *did* call me a maniac for having gone along with Bruce's crazy stunts, and he did tell me *he'd* never be so stupid as to risk *his* life unnecessarily. But other than that, he was perfect!"

Elizabeth laughed. "You know, Jess, now that it's all over, I can admit to you just how scared I was. I mean, I even called the teen hot line at Project Youth. I wanted to know if I should force you to quit Club X or if I should just leave you to your fate."

Jessica grinned. "You won't believe this, but *I* called, too!"

"You did? Somehow I never pictured you as the type to use the hot line." Elizabeth smiled. "I mean, what if you had gotten Amy?"

"I would have hung up in a second! But seriously, the person I spoke to was really helpful. She didn't give me any answers, or anything. And, I have to admit, at the time I was pretty annoyed about that. But now I know that she was trying to make me see that I had the answers all along. It was just a matter of my learning to listen to that little voice inside me. And to that big voice belonging to my older sister!"

Elizabeth laughed and reached for a sheet of paper on her desk. "Here," she said. "Read this. I'm doing an update article on the hot line. These are my notes. Any ideas?"

Jessica quickly scanned the paper. "Not really, Liz. You know I'm not much on the journalistic aspect of life. But you know who you should talk to? Denise Hadley. I heard Amy at lunch the other day trying to sell her on the idea of joining up. Denise didn't get a word in edgewise, but you know Amy. With the way her mouth goes, she could get a job recruiting for the army. She probably got Denise and her entire family to sign a lifetime commitment!"

"I wouldn't doubt it. You know, as annoying as Amy can still be, I really think her work on the hot line has changed her. Doesn't she strike you as a bit more sympathetic and, well, nicer?"

"I guess," Jessica responded. Then she yawned. "Sorry, Liz. But I suddenly feel totally and completely exhausted. I've got to crash."

Elizabeth stretched her arms over her head. "Me, too. I'll talk to Denise. And maybe Amy has some new information about the hot line, too. Thanks for the lead, Jess."

"No problem." Jessica stood up. "But you know Amy can't tell you any secrets about the people who call, don't you?"

"Of course. I *did* already do an article on the

hot line back when Amy first joined," Elizabeth reminded her sister.

Jessica yawned again. "Oh, yeah. Sorry, Liz. But I'd love to hear any good gossip you manage to get. I bet people actually fall in love over the phone! You know, girl in distress calls big strong boy who helps set her straight and she's eternally grateful . . ."

"Oh, please!" Elizabeth got up from her desk chair and pushed Jessica ahead of her out of the room. "Falling in love over the phone. Who ever heard of something so unlikely?"

Jessica grinned. "Or so romantic."

Will the teen hot line lead to love for someone at Sweet Valley High? Find out in Sweet Valley High 87, **MY BEST FRIEND'S BOYFRIEND.**